P9-CKU-031

"What did you want to discuss?" Joy asked.

"I had an idea for a fund-raiser. For years, people in this community have been curious about this property." Chase's eyes shone with his idea. "Why don't we have an event to honor the family's legacy and offer tours of the house? We could also have an ice-cream-and-lemonade social on the lawn."

"It's a wonderful idea. We'll need time to plan and advertise, but I think we could hold it the last weekend in July." Just before their eviction. Maybe, if they were successful with the fund-raiser, grants and other income sources, they wouldn't be evicted, after all.

The children returned with several long sticks and together, they helped the children roast their marshmallows.

When Chase looked at her, he smiled, and she remembered all the reasons she had fallen in love with him. He was confident, smart, kind and one of the most generous people she'd ever met—thankfully she also knew his faults, because if she didn't, she might find herself falling for him all over again.

Gabrielle Meyer lives in central Minnesota on the banks of the Mississippi River with her husband and four young children. As an employee of the Minnesota Historical Society, she fell in love with the rich history of her state and enjoys writing fictional stories inspired by real people and events. Gabrielle can be found at www.gabriellemeyer.com, where she writes about her passion for history, Minnesota and her faith.

Books by Gabrielle Meyer

Love Inspired

A Mother's Secret

Love Inspired Historical

A Mother in the Making
A Family Arrangement
Inherited: Unexpected Family
The Gift of Twins

A Mother's Secret

Gabrielle Meyer

LOVE INSPIRED

INSPIRATIONAL ROMANCE

If you purchased this book without a cover you should be aware that this book is stolen property. It was reported as "unsold and destroyed" to the publisher, and neither the author nor the publisher has received any payment for this "stripped book."

LOVE INSPIRED®
INSPIRATIONAL ROMANCE

Recycling programs for this product may not exist in your area.

ISBN-13: 978-1-335-48798-8

A Mother's Secret

Copyright ©2020 by Gabrielle Meyer

All rights reserved. No part of this book may be used or reproduced in any manner whatsoever without written permission except in the case of brief quotations embodied in critical articles and reviews.

This is a work of fiction. Names, characters, places and incidents are either the product of the author's imagination or are used fictitiously. Any resemblance to actual persons, living or dead, businesses, companies, events or locales is entirely coincidental.

This edition published by arrangement with Harlequin Books S.A.

For questions and comments about the quality of this book, please contact us at CustomerService@Harlequin.com.

Love Inspired
22 Adelaide St. West, 40th Floor
Toronto, Ontario M5H 4E3, Canada
www.Harlequin.com

Printed in U.S.A.

Religion that God our Father accepts
as pure and faultless is this: helping widows
and orphans in their distress.
—*James 1:27*

To my husband, David.

Chapter One

❧

A flood of memories filled Chase Asher as he unlocked the front door of his great-uncle's mansion, Bee Tree Hill. He hesitated to enter, not because anyone lived there, but because he hated to face the reminder of his past mistakes. Uncle Morgan was gone, the house was empty, but the memories, both good and bad, lingered.

Stepping over the threshold and into the walnut-paneled foyer, he forced the past to stay where it belonged and focused on the task ahead. His father wanted to sell the estate by the end of July, leaving Chase with just two months to inventory Uncle Morgan's things, fix any minor repairs and quietly grieve the passing of a man who was like a father to him. Thankfully, he'd have the place all to himself, a nice change from the chaotic office back in Seattle.

"One…two…three!" A child's voice cried out from the front parlor. "Ready, not, here I come!"

A little girl with dark brown pigtails and pink overalls ran out of the next room and right into Chase's leg. The child fell and bounced on her backside. She looked up at Chase with large, brown eyes. "Tag!" she said with a giggle. "You're it."

Chase stepped back, his pulse pounding hard. Where in the world had the child come from? The place was supposed to be empty. "Who are you?"

"Kinsley," she said, pointing to her chest.

She started to pick herself up off the ground, but Chase couldn't stand by and just watch. He picked her up and put her on her feet. "Are you hurt?"

"No." Her eyes turned into half crescents when she smiled. "I okay."

Another little girl, this one in purple overalls, came out of the powder room on Chase's right. She was an identical copy of Kinsley, with brown pigtails and brown eyes.

What was happening? Where were these kids coming from?

"And who are you?" Chase asked, a frown pulling his eyebrows together. Had someone been living here illegally? His uncle had been gone for only three weeks—enough time for someone to realize the house was empty. He hated to think he'd have to get the police involved, especially with the kids present.

The other little girl didn't answer, but ran toward the stairs at the opposite end of the foyer. "Mama!" she cried as her short legs worked overtime to climb the steps. "Mama!"

"That's Harper." Kinsley put her hands behind her back and bounced on her tiptoes, her pigtails swinging. "Who are you?"

"Chase Asher."

She stopped bouncing. "Grandpa Asher?"

Who was Grandpa Asher?

"You play hide, seek?" Kinsley didn't let Chase answer her first question, but took one of his fingers and pulled him toward the parlor. "You count." She let him go and ran through the parlor giggling. "Find me!"

Chase needed to discover who was squatting on his property, but first, he wanted to know who Grandpa Asher was to this little girl. Did she mean Uncle Morgan Asher?

He followed her through the parlor, into the fountain room, and turned left to enter the large music room. Windows along three walls let in a flood of daylight and revealed the plush landscape of the nine-acre estate just beyond the wavy glass. The Mississippi hugged the back side of the property and sparkled off in the distance.

It wasn't hard to find Kinsley. Her muffled giggles revealed that she was hiding behind an ornate sofa, her chubby hands covering her mouth.

Chase couldn't help but smile at the laughter and glee this child possessed—even if her parents were trespassers. How long had it been since he was so happy and carefree? "I found you," he said.

"You hide!" She jumped up and put her hands over her eyes. "One…two…"

"Who is Grandpa Asher?" Chase asked, crouching down. "Is he your grandpa?"

She uncovered her eyes and nodded. "My grandpa."

"Does he live here in Timber Falls?"

Kinsley shrugged.

How did he expect to get a straight answer from such a young child? Where were her parents?

"Can I help you?" A woman's voice pulled his attention away from the child.

He turned—and his heart stopped beating at the sight of Joy Gordon.

She stood at the top of the steps leading into the music room, Harper hugging her leg. A baseball bat was in her right hand, but when she met his gaze, it fell out of her hand and ricocheted off the wood floor. "Chase."

"Mama!" Kinsley ran around Chase and went to Joy, tugging on her T-shirt. "I'm hungry."

It took a minute for Chase's brain to catch up with the facts. Joy had children?

Twins?

He could hardly believe it.

"Go into the kitchen," Joy said to her daughters, disentangling Harper's hold on her leg. "Mrs. Thompson should have the afternoon snacks ready."

Chase used the distraction to rise and take a steadying breath.

He never expected to see Joy again—let alone here, in the very house where he'd fallen in love with her and then left her without an explanation. He thought she'd be long gone.

The girls ran off and Joy came down the steps. Distrust was written all over her face, and rightfully so. She had no reason to trust him again.

Her blond hair was pulled back in a messy bun and she wore a wrinkled T-shirt, but she was more attractive than he remembered. He had measured every woman he met in the past four years up against Joy's beauty—and found all of them lacking.

"What are you doing here?" she asked, her voice shaky.

"What am *I* doing here? I was just about to ask you the same question."

She didn't come close, but kept a considerable distance between them. "I live here."

"Since when?"

There was a quiet pause and then she said, "I never left."

"I thought you were just working here that summer. Uncle Morgan let you stay?"

"Yes."

"Why?"

Her eyebrows came together. "He wanted to help me."

Four years ago, Joy was going to a local college to be a school social worker. Uncle Morgan had hired her for the summer to do light cleaning to earn money for tuition. Chase had always assumed she graduated and went on to get a different job, maybe get married and start a family. By the looks of it, at least that part was true.

"Why did he want to help?" Chase wished he wasn't so confused right now. His father had told him the house was empty. Why hadn't someone informed him that Joy was still there?

She tugged at the hem of her T-shirt self-consciously. "Two years ago, I became a foster mom to three brothers. Since I was still living here helping, Uncle Morgan asked if I would like to live in the main house while he moved into the carriage house. He said the mansion was meant for a growing family to enjoy." She lifted a shoulder and shook her head. "I never asked him to move into the carriage house. He insisted."

Just like Uncle Morgan to give his home to a family— Joy's family.

Chase pointed toward the entrance, incredulity tinting his words. "Are the twins yours?" It was hard to think of Joy falling in love with someone else and starting a family.

Joy nodded, her dark brown gaze lowering to her hands. "They are."

A quiet pause punctuated their awkward conversation, but Chase finally managed to say, "They're beautiful."

She lifted her eyes again and studied him. "Thank you."

"Mama!" a boy called from the front of the house. "We're home!"

"School's all done for the summer!" cried another.

"Excuse me," Joy said as she walked away from Chase. "The boys are home."

He followed Joy out of the music room and back into the foyer. The boys were dropping backpacks, tennis shoes, folders and sports equipment on the Oriental rug, all talking at once.

"I'm hungry," the oldest one said. "Does Mrs. Thompson have cookies?"

"Yes." Joy picked up the things the boys were tossing on the ground. "But there will be no snacks until you've put all your things away. I want backpacks, folders and other school supplies on the dining room table so I can sort through them later." She handed the things back to the boys. "Your sporting equipment needs to go on the back porch—"

The boys grabbed their things and started to run off.

"I'm not finished," Joy said with the authority of a mom. "I want it all organized. Don't just throw it in there."

The boys all had blond hair and blue eyes, and were stair steps in height, each coming up to the chin of the next one older. They nodded that they understood, but continued on to the dining room.

"If you have any dirty laundry, please put it down the laundry chute. And wash your hands!" she called out.

The shortest boy, maybe six years old, stopped and frowned at Chase. "Who are you?"

"This is Mr. Asher," Joy said.

The boy looked up at Joy. "Did he know Grandpa Asher?"

"Who is Grandpa Asher?" Chase asked impatiently, recalling what Kinsley had said earlier.

"That's what they called your uncle," Joy said, a sad

smile in her voice. "He was a grandpa to the kids in every way."

"We miss him." The little boy's face pinched in grief for a moment, and then he ran toward the dining room, calling out to his brothers to wait for him.

Joy picked up some loose rubber bands and a stray paper clip on the rug.

"I can see why Uncle Morgan opened his home to you." Chase shook his head in amazement at what he'd just seen. Joy. A mom. A good mom. "You've got your hands full. I'm just surprised that my father didn't know you were here."

"Why are *you* here, Chase?" Joy set the office supplies on a nearby table and turned to him, questions in her eyes.

He wished he didn't have to tell her, but she'd have to learn the truth sometime. With a sigh he answered, "I came to sell Bee Tree Hill."

Joy put her hand over her mouth to try to hide her reaction. Sell the mansion?

"But—" She swallowed hard. "I—I thought Uncle Morgan told the Asher Corporation that he wished for the children and me to live here after his death."

Compassion filled Chase's eyes, but he didn't have any right to feel bad. Where was his compassion four years ago when he walked out on her? "My father didn't say anything about Uncle Morgan's wishes. And since the corporation owns the home, it's ours to sell."

At the mention of Chase's father, Joy flinched. Her only experience with the man was when he'd heard that Chase wanted to marry her. She'd been a poor college student who had grown up in one foster home after the next. When Chase's father had arrived, he confronted

Joy while she was cleaning a bathroom and told her she would never be good enough for his son. He accused her of using Chase for his family's money. While she knelt before a toilet, yellow rubber gloves on her hands, he told her he had given Chase an ultimatum, either he break things off with her, or lose his inheritance. When Chase left, without saying goodbye, Joy realized he had given her up for the money.

Of all the pain, rejection and disappointment she'd ever felt in her life, no one had demeaned her the way Chase's father had that day.

Now Joy paced away from Chase, her mind spinning with everything that had just happened in the last ten minutes, hoping Kinsley and Harper would stay out of sight. She didn't want him to ask any more questions about the twins. "What does this mean for the children and me? What about Mrs. Thompson? She's lived here most of her life working for your uncle. With Mr. Thompson gone, she's all alone in the world, and as far as I know, she doesn't have a retirement to live on. Where will all of us go?"

Chase ran his hands through his dark brown hair. It was still as wavy and unruly as ever. How many times had she run her own hands through his hair? The memory of how it felt made her fingers tingle, so she clenched them into fists. It had taken her a long time to get over Chase Asher and she wasn't about to dredge up those old memories again.

"I don't know." He shook his head. "I have to think. I didn't know you were here. I thought this would be an uncomplicated transaction. I'd just walk in, fix things up a little and oversee the sale."

Her heart pounded hard in her chest, but she kept her voice low. "I can't look my kids in the eyes and tell them they have to move—again. The boys lived in four different foster homes—and I don't know how many other places—before I brought them here two years ago. I told them I would do everything in my power to make sure they didn't have to move again."

"I don't know what to say, Joy—"

The door to the kitchen opened. "Is it you, Chase?" Mrs. Thompson's round cheeks were pink and her gray hair was pinned in a loose bun at the back of her head. Delight filled her eyes at the sight of Chase. "When Kodi told me Mr. Asher was here, and I heard that rich baritone voice of yours, I could hardly move fast enough to lay eyes on you again."

Chase extended his hand and walked toward her. "Hello, Mrs. Thompson."

She reached out and pulled him into her plump embrace. "Only a hug will do after four years apart." She squeezed him, her mouth working in a prayer of thanksgiving, no doubt. Mrs. Thompson made no excuses about her faith, and she was always the first to offer God thanksgiving for his many blessings.

But Joy didn't see Chase's arrival as a blessing. He had come to take away Bee Tree Hill, and, if she wasn't careful, he could take Kinsley and Harper, as well.

"I'm sorry I didn't make it home for Mr. Thompson's funeral," Chase said. "I—"

"No need to apologize," Mrs. Thompson said. "I received your beautiful card and flowers." She released him from the hug, but held on to his hands. She wasn't a very tall woman, so she had to look up at Chase, who stood at least six feet tall.

In the years since Chase left, his arms had grown more muscular, his shoulders had become broader, and his face had become more handsome, if that was possible. Was he married?

A quick look at his ring finger revealed no wedding band, but that didn't mean anything.

Chase glanced in Joy's direction and caught her looking him over. She dropped her gaze in embarrassment, wondering what he thought about her after all this time. Did she look more timeworn and stressed? Did the years of being a single mother show on her face? Was she as washed out as she felt? She had worked a half day at Timber Falls Elementary, where she was a social worker, and had come home, thrown on some black yoga pants and a T-shirt and was vacuuming bedrooms when Harper ran upstairs to tell her a stranger was in the house. She must look a fright.

"What are you doing here, boy?" Mrs. Thompson asked Chase.

"Unfortunately," Chase let out a breath, "I came to Bee Tree Hill to get it ready to sell."

Mrs. Thompson's smile fell and she searched his face. "Sell Bee Tree Hill?"

Chase nodded, his eyebrows tilting together. "I'm sorry, Mrs. Thompson. It's not my choice. The board met just a week ago and made the decision. I was sent to oversee the details."

Mrs. Thompson nodded slowly. "I understand." She patted Chase's cheek and winked. "A man's heart deviseth his way: but the Lord directeth his steps. We'll let the good Lord figure this one out for us. Now," she put her hands on her hips, "where will you stay?"

"I thought I'd be staying here." He shrugged and glanced at Joy again. "But, under the circumstances, I don't think it would be best. I can go to a hotel."

A hotel as far away from Bee Tree Hill as possible.

"Nonsense." Mrs. Thompson grinned. "You can stay above the carriage house, just like your uncle Morgan was doing. He had the place updated just a couple years ago when Joy and the kids moved in here. I cleaned it myself right after he went into the hospital last month, so the place should work just fine for you."

Chase searched Joy's face for her approval. "Would that work?"

If she had her choice, she would say no. But it wasn't her place to make that decision. He represented the rightful owners. "That's fine."

He nodded. "I'll get my things out of the rental car and be out of your way—"

"No, you won't." Mrs. Thompson took his arm as Chase was about to turn away. "You'll stay here for supper and we'll have a nice long visit before you head down to the carriage house later."

Joy stepped forward to protest the invitation, but Chase responded faster than her.

"I don't want to impose," he said.

He didn't want to impose? Joy almost snorted. His very presence in the house was the biggest imposition of her life. What was she going to do? How would she keep the girls' identity a secret from him? All he would need to do was find out how old they were and he'd probably guess. They were small for their age, so he might think they were younger than three—but if he asked them, they'd tell him the truth.

"Fiddlesticks," Mrs. Thompson laughed. "I'll leave you and Joy to chat for a bit while I get the kids their snacks." With that, she disappeared back into the kitchen, closing the door soundly.

Joy's mind raced with all the implications of Chase's arrival, but there was only one thing she could focus on.

She would do whatever it would take to keep the house for the kids, and protect her girls from Chase's family.

He sighed as he faced Joy. "I'm going to see what I can do about this mess. If the board knew you and the kids were here, I don't think they would have sent me. Somehow, Uncle Morgan's wishes were not made known to the corporation."

Hope sprung up in Joy's heart at his words. "Do you think there's a way we could still keep the house?"

"I'll see what I can do. I'll call my father and tell him what happened."

It wasn't much, but at least Chase was willing to do what he could. A part of her wanted to believe he would do the right thing, while the other part remembered how much pain he had caused her when he walked away without an explanation. A couple weeks after he left, when she had found out she was pregnant, she had tried to contact him, but he never returned her calls. Eventually, the number was disconnected. After she learned she was expecting twins, the desire to protect her babies from the Asher family had overwhelmed her, so she had kept her secret. If they knew the girls existed, what would stop them from fighting for custody? They had a fortune at their fingertips and she was a single mother who didn't even own the home she lived in.

Thankfully, Uncle Morgan had let her stay on at Bee Tree Hill while she went to school, and Mrs. Thompson had helped with childcare once they were born. Both Uncle Morgan and Mrs. Thompson had wanted Joy to tell Chase the truth, but she had kept putting it off—and made them promise not to tell.

But now? Now she might be homeless and would have no excuse left to keep the girls' identity from their father.

"I appreciate whatever you can do to help," Joy told .

Chase, forcing herself not to think about the inevitable conversation they must have. For now, they had other things to worry about.

Chapter Two

Chase pulled his phone from his back pocket and stepped out the front door of the house. Bright sunshine filtered through the massive pine trees lining the circle drive. An old tennis court and pool house sat on the sprawling front lawn, and stone pathways crisscrossed over the property, leading down the hill at the back of the mansion to the river beyond. Why had Chase waited so long to return to Bee Tree Hill? He had been in Italy on business when he got word that Uncle Morgan had passed. It had been impossible to get a flight home on such short notice, so he had missed the funeral. He should have made a point to come back to visit before Uncle Morgan died, even if it meant facing his past mistakes.

He walked to a double gliding swing and sat, tapping the phone icon on his screen. He found his father's number and pressed Call.

It rang several times and then his father answered. "Did you have any trouble getting in?"

"Hi, Dad." Chase could imagine his father sitting in his office in downtown Seattle, mist outside the large windows, and a view of the Space Needle not too far away.

"What do you need, Chase?"

Taking a deep breath, he rose from the swing, not able to stay still. "We have a problem."

There was a pause. "What kind of problem?"

Chase didn't want to tell his father that Joy was the one living in the house. If he knew who it was, he would probably call Chase home and send someone else to deal with the situation.

"Apparently, Uncle Morgan had moved into the carriage house a couple years ago and was letting a woman live in the mansion. She's a foster mom and has five kids. Mrs. Thompson is still living here, too, helping with the kids."

"What's the problem?"

Chase rubbed the tension in the back of his neck as he paced across the manicured lawn. "She told me that Uncle Morgan wanted her to stay here, even after his death."

"I'm sure she did." Dad's sarcastic words were flat and devoid of emotion. "Tell her she has a week to vacate the premises."

"I can't do that."

Dead silence on the other end of the phone wasn't a good sign.

The boys ran out of the house, shouting and hollering in excitement as they disappeared around the corner of the mansion. Chase moved in that direction, drawn to their enthusiasm.

"The mom has nowhere to go," Chase continued. "Not to mention Mrs. Thompson. She's lived here for at least thirty years. Where will she go?"

"That's not my problem. My grandfather built Bee Tree Hill and when he died, he left the estate to the corporation. We allowed Uncle Morgan to live there, because it was the only home he'd ever known. Now that he's dead and there are no other Ashers living in Timber

Falls, we can finally sell the estate. I won't let a woman and her kids dictate what we do with the place."

Uncle Morgan had shared the history of the estate with Chase when he'd stayed with him four years ago. Chase's great-great-grandfather was a lumber baron in Illinois who had sent each of his sons to a different location in the Western United States to build sawmills in the 1890s. He sent John, Chase's great-grandfather, to Timber Falls, Minnesota, and that's when John built Bee Tree Hill. Uncle Morgan was one of John's sons. He was born and raised in the mansion, and had chosen to stay when the rest of the family moved to Seattle where the company was now headquartered. The property had been part of the family legacy for over a century and it seemed like a shame to sell it now, but it wasn't up to Chase.

"It's going to take me at least a month to get the place ready to sell," Chase said, trying to buy time for Joy and the kids. "I need to have an appraiser look at a hundred years' worth of antiques and collectibles, not to mention all the work that needs to be done around here. It could take another month or so to find a buyer after that. Why can't we let her stay until we sell the place? Timber Falls is a small town. It would look bad for the corporation if we kicked out a foster mom, her five kids and an old woman with little warning."

Dad hated looking bad. It was the reason he had stepped in when he heard Chase wanted to marry Joy. One of the first things he said to Chase was, "What would it look like if you married a woman who grew up in foster care?" He had different plans for Chase, which included marrying the daughter of one of his business partners. But Chase had messed that up, too. Tamara was tired of waiting for Chase to set a wedding date after being engaged for three years, so she left him just before he went to Italy. It wasn't even two months since their breakup and she had already become engaged to someone else.

"Fine." Dad's voice was louder than it needed to be. "She can stay, but only until the end of July. That should give her plenty of time to find a place to live."

Relief filled Chase. At least Joy had two months to figure out a different plan. He took the stone steps down the hill, toward the river and the sound of the boys playing. "What about Mrs. Thompson?"

"I don't care about the staff." Dad was the president and CEO of the Asher Corporation and he'd earned his way to the top by being a hard-nosed businessman. His lack of empathy was famous in the Asher family, but very few people understood it as well as Chase. "She should have planned better," Dad said. "Let her stay until the end of July, too, but not a day longer. And keep an eye on all of them. Once they know they're being evicted, they'll probably start selling off the antiques."

Chase had nothing but respect for Joy and Mrs. Thompson and he knew they would never stoop so low. "I will."

"Chase."

"Yeah?"

"Don't mess this up, too. It's an easy job. That's why I sent you to do it." His father hung up without a goodbye.

Chase lowered his phone and stared at the home screen for a second. His parents had divorced years ago, and his mother hardly spoke to his father anymore. Chase's aunts, uncles and cousins also kept their distance. The only person who spoke to Malcolm, besides Chase, was his aunt Constance. She and Uncle Morgan had been siblings. She was the last family member from that generation to remain alive and she took it upon herself to remind Malcolm—and the rest of the family—where they came from.

What would it be like to have a father he could lean on for support or a word of wisdom? Aunt Constance said Dad wasn't always this way. His love of money and power had turned him into a ruthless man. He wanted Chase to take over the business one day, but if Chase followed in his steps, would he become like his dad?

The day he had walked away from Joy, he suspected he had the ability to become ruthless. But how did he stop the trajectory of his life, when he wanted to please his father, despite all the pain and heartache his father had caused?

Chase found the boys near a large basswood tree, a pile of old lumber sitting at the base, and another pile nailed to the tree in a dangerous, haphazard way. The oldest boy had a handful of nails and one of the smaller boys held a hammer.

"What are you boys doing?" Chase asked, his hands in his pockets.

"Building a tree fort," the smallest one said. "Did you ever build a tree fort?"

Chase hadn't spent much time playing outside as a kid. In the summer, when most boys were building tree forts, he was inside with a tutor, hired to teach him French and trigonometry. His father wanted him to be the smartest student in his class, but all Chase wanted was freedom to play like a normal kid. "No, but I always wanted one."

"Do you like our fort?" The oldest pointed up into the tree.

Chase tried to keep his face from showing his real thoughts about the mess in the tree. "That looks a little dangerous."

"It's okay, if we're careful." The boy started to climb

a makeshift ladder they had nailed into one of the trunks of the massive tree. The strip of wood spun and his foot slipped off.

"I think you better not climb up there." Chase was tall enough to push on one of the boards. It dislodged and fell between the trunks. "Does your mom know you're building this?"

The oldest boy shrugged.

"Did you tell her?"

"No."

"Will you help us?" the youngest asked, his blue eyes wide with hope.

Chase had a hundred things he needed to do, but none of it sounded half as fun as building a tree fort. The boys had a couple months left at Bee Tree Hill, why not give them good memories while he could? "We can ask your mom if it's okay at supper. If she says yes, then we can make our plans for a proper tree fort."

The boys cheered and dropped all their supplies.

"Let's go now," said the oldest.

"We can wait for supper." Chase smiled at the kids, their enthusiasm contagious. "I don't even know your names."

"I'm Ryan," said the oldest. "I'm eight. Jordan is seven, and Kodi is six."

"I'm Chase." He wasn't sure if Joy wanted them to call him Mr. Asher, but he didn't want to sound so formal. People called his dad Mr. Asher. "I'll be living in the carriage house for a while."

"Come on, Chase." Kodi took his hand and tugged him toward the barn on the south end of the property. For some reason, his fingers were covered in chocolate. "We'll show you where we got the wood."

He let go of Chase's hand and took off running down

the road that led around the base of the hill. Ryan and Jordan trailed after their little brother, glancing over their shoulders to make sure Chase was following.

It was bad enough forcing Joy and Mrs. Thompson out of their home, but even worse evicting kids. There had to be a way to keep them all at Bee Tree Hill.

He owed it to Joy to at least try.

The aroma of Mrs. Thompson's famous lasagna and garlic bread wafted through the house as Joy picked up the coloring books and crayons the girls had left on the dining room table. She had sent them off to the kitchen to wash up for dinner when she had caught sight of Chase walking toward the house with the boys.

Several things had distracted him when he first arrived, and he probably hadn't had time to think about Kinsley and Harper's age, or the fact that they had his nose and hair. She'd come to accept that it would be impossible to keep them away from Chase forever. If he suspected he was their father and asked, she wouldn't lie, but she wasn't quite ready to tell him, either.

"Mama?" Kodi ran into the house, his big brothers close on his heels. He was the youngest of the boys, but he usually led the way. "Can we build a tree fort with Chase?"

Chase followed the boys into the dining room, his hair windblown and his eyes sparkling.

Joy's breath caught at the sight of him and it took her a moment to compose her thoughts. Why did he have to be so good-looking?

"I'm sure Mr. Asher has enough to keep busy." Joy set the coloring books and crayons in a built-in hutch. The dining room, just like the rest of the house, still retained its historic flavor. Thick trim, painted a creamy white, dominated the room, while a chandelier hung over the long walnut table. She kept a tablecloth on it at all times to protect it from the inevitable scratches and dents the kids would inflict on the expensive wood. All the rooms in the house were full of Asher family heirlooms, and it was a full-time job keeping them safe from the kids.

"They can call me Chase," he said, but then added quickly, "if that's okay with you."

It wasn't okay with her. She'd rather he keep a professional distance from the kids. But one look at their expectant faces and she knew it was already too late.

"Can we build the fort?" Ryan asked, his freckles already becoming more prominent from the sunshine and being outside during the warmer weather. "Chase said he'd help, but we had to ask you first."

Joy searched Chase's face. He almost looked as excited and eager as the boys. "Would you like to build them a tree fort?"

He nodded, his mouth tilting up in a smile. "I would."

"It'll be better than the one we built," Ryan said with assurance.

How could she say no to this request? The boys didn't have many male role models in their life—and though she would have chosen someone other than Chase, it seemed that God had brought him here.

Hopefully not for long.

"Did you speak to your father?" she asked Chase.

"Mama!" the three boys called out impatiently.

"Can we build a fort?" Jordan asked.

It didn't pay to fight them. She put her hands on Jordan's cheeks and smiled down into his adorable little face. "You can build your tree fort, but only when Mr. Asher has time. Don't bug him if he's busy." She knew how persistent these children could be. They would drive him crazy if she didn't stop them.

"Yes!" Ryan pumped his fist in the air and the other two tried to mimic him.

"Now go wash up for supper." She ruffled Kodi's hair as he ran past.

The door between the butler's pantry and the dining room swung on its hinge after the boys rushed through. It squeaked mercilessly.

Chase walked over to the door and opened and closed it a few times. "I'd be happy to fix this for you."

It had been making that noise for weeks, and Joy would be grateful to have it fixed, but she didn't want Chase in the house, if she could help it. "I can take care of it."

"It's why I came, Joy." He went to the French doors that led from the fountain room into the dining room and ran his hand over a piece of trim that had come loose. "If you have time tomorrow, I'd like to go through the whole house and make a list of the minor repairs that need attention. If there's something major, I'll call a professional."

Joy was conscious of being alone with Chase, even if her kids and Mrs. Thompson were on the other side of the butler's pantry. While Chase had called his father, she had run up to her room, pulled her hair out of the messy bun, changed into some cuffed jeggings and put on a nice shirt. She'd even touched up her makeup and slipped on a pair of sandals. She told herself she had done it because he was a guest, and she usually tried to look nice when she entertained—but she knew she had done it because there was still a part of her that didn't feel worthy of Chase Asher. It was a part that had been with her since she was a child in her first foster home. She was always viewed as the dirty, unlovable kid that no one wanted. When Chase left her, it only confirmed that belief.

"I didn't realize you were the handy type," Joy said, wanting to change the course of her thoughts. She was now a respectable adult, raising a houseful of kids. She didn't have anything to prove to anyone.

He smiled as he continued around the dining room inspecting the trim, the windows, even the wallpaper. "When I was here last time—" He paused and glanced at her, regret on his face. "About that, Joy. I'd like to explain why—"

She lifted her hand to stop him. "Please don't." There was nothing he could say to make up for what he had done to her. She'd rather they not discuss it.

Chase let out a long sigh. "Mr. Thompson took me under his wing that summer and taught me a lot. I helped him with several projects and found I had the knack for handiwork. You can trust me."

Trust him. How could she ever trust him again?

"Dinner's ready." Mrs. Thompson poked her head into the dining room. "Come and get it."

"Aren't we eating in here?" Chase asked.

Joy wrinkled her nose. "We prefer to eat in the kitchen. The dining room feels too formal."

She led him into the butler's pantry and through another swinging door into the kitchen. The room wasn't overly large, but it was big enough for a table and chairs. A large window looked out at the river, displaying the late evening sun glistening off the water.

"It smells delicious, Mrs. Thompson." Chase went to the sink and washed his hands. "I remember your lasagna well."

Mrs. Thompson grinned. "I thought you would. I once made a pan, just for you." Her eyes grew wide when she looked at the children. "And he ate the *whole thing* in one sitting!"

"Whoa!" Ryan said, clearly impressed by such a feat.

"Hello again," Chase said to Harper and Kinsley, who were seated in their booster chairs at the table, large bibs covering their pink and purple overalls.

Joy held her breath while her pulse ticked in her wrists. Would he recognize them as his daughters now?

"Sit here," Kinsley ordered Chase, pointing to the chair beside her.

"Please," Joy reminded her, watching Chase closely. If he had any suspicions, he didn't show them.

"I'd be happy to sit beside you," Chase answered, "but you better not try to steal my lasagna."

Kinsley's dimpled grin lit up her face. "I eat all your lasagna!"

"Not if I can help it." Chase laughed with the little girl and Joy's heart squeezed at the sight. From the moment she knew the girls were on their way, to this moment now, she had always wondered what it would have been like if Chase had chosen her over his family money. All throughout her uncertain pregnancy, while she was giving birth and in the long months afterward when she was trying to finish college and get a job, she had been so angry at him. As a child, she had promised herself a different life for her children than the one she had been dealt—yet here she was, a single woman, trying to do the work of both mom and dad. She couldn't even guarantee a place for the kids to live.

Harper sat across the table from Kinsley and Chase, uncertainty in her dark brown eyes. She was the least likely of Joy's children to embrace a stranger, but when she allowed someone into her heart, she held on to them fiercely. Joy had witnessed it in the Sunday school classroom, in her preschool classroom and in their interactions with neighbors and friends. Would Harper ever embrace Chase?

"Hello, Harper." Chase must have noticed the little girl's frown as she stared at him.

Harper didn't respond, but put her head down on her folded arms.

The food was already on the table, so Joy took a seat beside Harper and laid her hand on her back. "Harper is just a little shy around strangers," she tried to explain—though why she felt the need to clarify anything to Chase was a mystery to her. After the way he had left her, he deserved very little from her or the children.

"Let's say grace." Joy took Harper's and Jordan's hands and bowed her head, but she kept her eyes open to see how Chase would handle praying with the family. When he had been in Timber Falls the last time, they had spent hours talking about their questions concerning God. It wasn't until after the girls were born, and Mrs. Thompson had introduced Joy to the members of her church, that Joy had embraced her faith. Had Chase become a believer, too?

He didn't hesitate, but took Kinsley's hand in one and Ryan's hand in the other. He also bowed his head, but caught her watching him before he closed his eyes. His smile was soft and gentle, but it made her cheeks burn.

Closing her eyes tight, she prayed, "Lord, thank You for this meal, this family and all Your provisions. Amen."

"And thank You for Chase," Kodi added quickly. "And the tree fort he's going to build us."

"Amen," everyone else echoed.

"Tree fort?" Kinsley's eyes grew wide. "I come to your tree fort?"

"No, Kinney, you're too little," Kodi told her as he took a piece of bread from the basket passing by.

"I not too little!" She frowned indignantly, crossing her arms.

Chase smiled. "Would you like some salad, Miss Kinsley?"

Her frown deepened and she wrinkled her nose. "Carrots are yucky."

"Then pick them out," Joy told her daughter.

Kinsley started to pick out the carrot sticks on her plate. While Chase was helping Jordan, she quietly set the offensive vegetables on Chase's plate.

"What's this?" Chase asked when he finished with Jordan. He hadn't placed anything on his plate yet, so the carrots were obviously not his.

Kinsley took a bite out of her garlic bread. "They're yucky."

"Then why would I want them?" he asked.

"Because you're an adult," Kodi supplied, as if the answer was obvious. "And adults eat their vegetables. Right, Mom?"

Joy nodded, hiding a smile. "Kids should eat their vegetables, too."

A chorus of complaints filled the kitchen and then the conversation shifted in a dozen different directions. Since Chase was new to the kids, he was the center of their attention, and he answered all their questions patiently.

Joy watched him interact with the kids while a deep sadness overtook her. Why couldn't things have been different? Why had he told her he loved her four years ago, when he didn't plan to stick around and prove it to her? Were they just flowery words, used to get what he wanted?

It didn't matter anymore. She had learned her lesson. She'd never trust Chase Asher again.

Chapter Three

"It's getting late," Mrs. Thompson said as she set her coffee cup in the sink. "Here I've been, talking your ear off, and you're probably tired from all your traveling today." She set her hand on Chase's shoulder as she took his dirty plate. "You should head on down to the carriage house and get some sleep."

The sooner he was out of the mansion, the better. Joy stood and took her plate to the sink. The kids were watching TV in the front parlor while Mrs. Thompson and Chase had visited. Over the past thirty minutes, she had discovered that Chase graduated from the University of California, Los Angeles, the year after he left Timber Falls, had gone on to work with his father directly after college and was now living in Seattle. When Mrs. Thompson had asked if there was a special lady in his life, he had evaded the question and changed the subject.

Was there someone else in his life now? Did that someone know he was in Timber Falls with the mother of his children at this very moment?

Joy checked her thoughts and forced herself to stop thinking about Chase's love life.

"Let me help clear the table," Chase said.

"Nonsense." Mrs. Thompson took a dirty glass out of his hand. "I'll call the kids back in and they can help with the dishes. You should go with Joy and she'll show you around the carriage house."

The sun had already set, so the last streaks of daylight were splayed against the sky in pinks and purples. If she wanted to get him settled before it grew completely dark, they'd need to hurry. She'd prefer to send him there alone, but she still didn't know how his conversation had gone with his father and she hadn't wanted to ask in front of the children or Mrs. Thompson. If it hadn't gone well, she'd find a way to tell them herself.

"I'll grab the keys to the carriage house, if you want to drive your car down the hill," she said to Chase.

He nodded and cleared another plate off the table, despite Mrs. Thompson's protests. "Thank you for the delicious meal."

The older lady's cheeks glowed at the praise. "Anytime."

While Chase went out to his car, Joy grabbed the keys from a drawer in the foyer.

Stepping outside, she inhaled the fresh scent of early summer. Ducks quacked in a nearby pond, birds chirped from the treetops and squirrels pranced around the lawn. Deep green foliage filled in the space between branches, offering lushness to the great outdoors.

She walked down the hill to the white carriage house at the bottom and waited for Chase to park his rented Jeep Wrangler. The canvas top was down and he looked every bit the carefree son of a millionaire.

What would he think of her silver minivan, with dried french fries and cheesy fish crackers littering the floor? They were definitely living in two different worlds.

He jumped out of the Jeep and took his suitcase from the back seat.

"It's amazing how little this place has changed," he said as he followed her up the steep set of stairs outside the carriage house. The apartment was on the upper level, while the original carriages were stored in the garage on the main level. When Uncle Morgan had lived here, they had installed a chair lift to take him up and down the stairs, though he didn't leave the house often.

"Why change something that's already perfect?" she asked.

"I couldn't agree more." His voice had dropped an octave and Joy forced herself not to assume a deeper meaning behind his words.

When she reached the top of the steps, she unlocked the door and pushed it open. The apartment was dark, but she knew her way around. She and the kids had visited Uncle Morgan often, and he was always ready to hear about their lives. The place wasn't the same without him.

She flipped on the light switch as they stepped into the kitchen.

"Here are the keys." Joy turned and found Chase right behind her—much too close. She took a step back and handed him the keys. Their fingertips brushed against each other and she pulled away quickly. She remembered his touch all too well. "You should have everything you need," she went on. "We didn't move anything out after Uncle Morgan died, so you'll find all the necessities." Joy started to step around him to leave the apartment.

"Are you going?" he asked, setting his suitcase on the tile floor. "I had hoped to talk to you about the conversation with my dad."

How had she forgotten so quickly? "Okay."

He pulled one of the chairs out from the table. "Why don't you sit down?"

Joy did as he asked and took the seat. Unease crept into her stomach as she watched him settle into the chair opposite her. Why didn't he just get it over with? Tell her what she was dealing with.

"My father agreed to let you stay until the end of July." Chase's forehead wrinkled in dismay as he spoke to her. "I told him what you said about Uncle Morgan's wishes, but he won't budge." He swallowed and reached across the table to touch Joy's hand.

She pulled away, like she had just been burned.

Chase nodded, as if he understood that he had no right to touch her anymore. "He wanted to give you a week, but I talked him into letting you stay for two months."

Joy couldn't sit. Standing, she walked over to the counter and turned to face him. Had he fought hard for them, or simply given in to his father again? "I love Bee Tree Hill." She looked down at the floor, afraid she might cry. It was the last thing she wanted. She'd told herself years ago she would never let someone else see her pain. They just used it to hurt her. "I've lived here longer than I've lived anywhere in my life—and the kids—" She couldn't continue.

Chase rose from his chair and crossed the room. "I'm sorry, Joy. If I had a choice, I'd let you and the kids stay here forever."

His words and voice were so genuine, she almost believed he cared. But she knew better.

She moved away from him again and stood by the sink. "There has to be a way we can keep Bee Tree Hill."

"I wish there was, but I have no choice. I have to put it up for sale."

"Why can't I buy it?"

He frowned. "You?"

Indignation rose in her gut. "Why not?"

"Joy, it's worth millions of dollars. Do you have that kind of cash?"

"Of course not—but it's not impossible." Her mind started to race with possibilities. "I can apply for grants, ask service organizations for donations, hold fund-raisers and apply for a loan." If she'd learned anything in life, she had learned how to fight for what she wanted. "If you give me enough time, I can come up with the money."

"I don't know…"

"Just give me a chance. I have to try."

He didn't look convinced, but he nodded. "If you think you can do it…"

"I know I can." She crossed the room and turned when she got to the door. Desperation tinged her voice, but she didn't care. She had to fight for Bee Tree Hill. If she didn't, she couldn't face her kids. "I'll do everything in my power to raise enough money."

"I still have a job to do here," Chase said. "My father is expecting reports, so I'm going to have an appraiser come in and let me know what everything is worth. I'm also going to make all the necessary repairs and go through Uncle Morgan's personal items."

"I know." She didn't care what Chase had to do. All she cared about was raising the money. "And I'll meet with you tomorrow to go through the house and grounds to make a list of repairs." She needed to reassure him that she wouldn't be a hindrance to him, but would cooperate. If she was amiable and easy to work with, maybe he could convince his father to lower the price for the property—or give her more time. Anything would help.

"Okay." His smile looked sad and it made his blue

eyes soften at the corners. "I hope you raise the money, Joy. I wouldn't want anyone else to own Bee Tree Hill."

His words brought a lump to her throat and she turned to leave. She was going to cry and she couldn't let him see.

The next afternoon, Chase sat in the Jeep outside the mansion as he waited for Joy. Sunshine warmed his shoulders, while the breeze off the river was just enough to keep him from getting too hot. Up above, the tops of the pine trees swayed in the wind, while white cumulus clouds drifted by in the bright blue sky.

He had forgotten how much he loved Minnesota in the summer, especially here in Timber Falls, where life had a slower pace and neighbors still took the time to visit one another. Back in Seattle, he hardly knew the names of the people who lived in his apartment building, and he never visited with them. It was strange if they shared more than a brief hello in the hallway.

"Sorry." Joy stepped out of the house and came to the Jeep, her purse over her shoulder. "I had a harder time than usual putting Kinsley down for a nap. I try not to leave all five children with Mrs. Thompson, unless the girls are sleeping."

She grabbed the roll bar and pulled herself into the Jeep. He was astonished all over again that this young, attractive woman was the mother of five children. She was trim, stylish and had more energy than anyone he'd ever met. Her dark blond hair was a little longer than he remembered, but still as silky and thick. She tucked one side of it behind her ear like she used to, and let the rest fall over her shoulders.

A memory from their summer together hit him like it was yesterday. They had taken a picnic basket to the riverside and spent hours lying on a blanket, watching the water flow by, talking about what they wanted out of life. Chase had run his fingers through her hair as it lay splayed on the blanket and she had smiled up at him, love, trust and hope in her beautiful brown eyes. And that's when he knew he had wanted to marry her. Later that evening, he had called his father to tell him he wouldn't be returning to Seattle after graduation that year. He had wanted to marry Joy and move to Timber Falls.

But Dad had other plans, and he was in Timber Falls less than twenty-four hours later, giving Chase the ultimatum.

"Do you remember how to find the hardware store?" Joy asked, looking over the list they had compiled earlier.

Chase pulled his mind out of the past and nodded. "I went there almost every day with Mr. Thompson." He put the Jeep in Drive and pulled out of the estate. The top of the vehicle was still down and the wind pushed and tugged at them.

"Thanks for inviting me to come with you and help choose the paint." Joy held her hair back with her right hand. "I know you didn't have to."

Several of the rooms in the house hadn't seen a fresh coat of paint in years, so Chase had invited Joy along to pick out the colors she liked. If it was up to him, he would have chosen white for everything. Even if they were only there for a couple more months, he wanted Joy and the kids to feel at home.

"I don't know what color to get for Kinsley and Harper's room," she said with a sigh. "Kinsley insists on pink and Harper on purple."

Chase couldn't help but smile. It was easy to tell the girls apart that morning when he'd joined them for breakfast, because they were dressed the same as the day before, except this time, they weren't wearing overalls, but matching sundresses. Pink for Kinsley, purple for Harper.

"You can't change the color of their clothes, or I'll never get them straight." Chase took a left onto Main Street, the sight of the stately brick buildings bringing back even more memories.

"I've bought everything in those two colors." Joy's hair continued to blow in the wind, giving her a wild, carefree look. "If one of them decides to like yellow or green, I'll be in trouble."

Chase was quiet for a moment as he thought about the twins. Of all the things that had surprised him these past couple of days, Joy's twin daughters were the biggest shock. They had her brown eyes and her heart-shaped mouth, but those were the only features they shared with their mom. Yesterday, he hadn't thought too much about their father, but today, the thought had crossed his mind several times. Was Joy still in a relationship with him? If she was, no one had mentioned it. Had the dad skipped out on her? Was he still part of their lives?

It wasn't his place to ask her such a personal question, especially if the breakup was painful, but he couldn't help but wonder. Would she open up about it, if he asked?

Joy waved at several people along Main Street and one older gentleman shouted a hello as they turned onto Broadway. The sun reflected off the large plate glass windows on several buildings. A bakery, a bookstore, a woman's clothing store and more filled the charming downtown. Colorful flower baskets hung from historic streetlights and cast-iron benches were positioned along the tree-lined street.

At the hardware store, it took them over an hour to select paint and find all the necessary supplies to make repairs on their list. They carried doorknobs, hinges, light

switches and plaster out to the Jeep when they were finished.

"Is the West Side Café still open?" Chase asked Joy
after they secured their purchases in the back seat.

"Of course." She repositioned a can of paint. "It's the
most popular restaurant in town."

"I have been craving their stuffed hash browns and
biscuits and gravy for years." Just the thought of them
made his stomach growl. "How about an early supper?"

She paused as she climbed into the Jeep. Her face grew
serious and she shook her head. "I don't think that's a
good idea, Chase."

He got into the driver's seat, but didn't put the keys in
the ignition. "Why not?"

She sat and clasped her hands on her lap. "It's too
complicated."

Chase put his hands on the steering wheel and studied
the bricks on the building ahead of him. He didn't want
to go another step further until he apologized to her, but
how could he put into words the regret he felt? There
was no way to explain his actions—or any excuse that
could possibly make up for the heartache he was sure
she had endured. The only thing he could think to say
was, "I'm sorry."

She didn't respond, but stayed motionless in the seat
next to him.

He faced her. "There's nothing I can say—"

"No." She swallowed. "There's not, so please don't
even try."

"But I have to. I was young and stupid—not to mention scared." His words sounded flat, even to himself.
"I know that's not an excuse, but it's the truth. If I could
go back—"

"What?" She finally looked at him. "What would you

do differently? Stay? Stand up to your father?" She put up her hand. "No. Don't answer me. I don't want to know. I'd prefer to just focus on the present and what I need to do to keep Bee Tree Hill for my children."

"Joy?" A tall man approached the Jeep wearing a black pinstripe suit and a red tie. He wore shiny black shoes and dark sunglasses, and carried a briefcase.

"Tom." Joy got out of the Jeep and met him in the parking lot. They embraced and when Joy pulled away, she had a beautiful smile on her face. "When did you get back?"

"Last night." He took off his sunglasses and grinned at Joy. "I was going to call when I got home, but it was too late. And then this morning, I had an early hearing. I was just entering the courthouse when I saw you." He held her at arm's length. "You look great."

Joy dipped her head and continued to smile. "You look good yourself. The Florida sun agrees with you."

Chase stepped out of the Jeep, tired of being ignored, and extended his hand to Joy's friend. "I'm Chase."

"I'm sorry." Joy motioned to Chase. "Tom Winston, this is Chase Asher—Morgan Asher's great-nephew."

Tom's eyebrows came up. "This is Chase?"

Chase clenched his jaw at the question, but Joy simply nodded.

"It's nice to finally meet you." Tom shook Chase's hand with a steel-like grip. "What brings you back to town?"

Chase hated to say why he came, but he had little other choice. "I'm here on behalf of the Asher Corporation to sell Bee Tree Hill."

Tom's smile fell and he looked at Joy. "Did you know this was going to happen?"

She shook her head. "I thought Uncle Morgan made

his wishes known to the corporation, but apparently he didn't." Her mouth thinned. "And, if he did, I doubt his wishes would be honored."

It was a dig to Chase's family, but it was probably true.

"Do you want me to check and see if there's anything you can do from a legal standpoint?" Tom asked. "I'm willing to do whatever it takes for you and the kids."

Joy put her hand on Tom's arm and smiled. "I know you are, but I don't think there's much you can do this time."

Tom's face was serious as he looked deep into Joy's eyes. "If you'd only give me the word, I'd be by your side. You know I'd go to the moon and back for you and the kids."

Chase narrowed his gaze as he studied Tom's face. Was there a resemblance between him and the twins?

"Tom." Joy glanced at Chase, her cheeks turning pink. Was she embarrassed that Chase heard Tom?

"I ask her to marry me about every six months since she told me she was pregnant with the girls." Tom pulled Joy to his side and put his arm around her, but he looked at Chase. "Maybe you can convince her to say yes to me."

She put her hand on Tom's chest and playfully pushed him away. "You only ask me because you feel sorry for me."

"Your words hurt, Joy." Tom grinned, but then he grew serious again. "And you know that's not true."

An awkward silence came between them and Chase stepped over to the Jeep to open the door for Joy. "We should probably get back. Mrs. Thompson will be wondering why we've been gone so long."

"Are you staying at Bee Tree Hill?" Tom asked Chase.

"In the carriage house," Joy supplied as she got into the Jeep and closed the door. The window had been rolled down, so she put her elbow on the ledge and reached out to take Tom's hand. "Come by sometime soon. The kids miss you."

Tom wrapped both his hands around Joy's. "I will. And I'll see if I can do something about the estate."

"Thanks." She waved as Chase jumped into the Jeep and started the engine.

For some reason, knowing who possibly fathered Kinsley and Harper didn't fill Chase with relief. Instead, it made him more uneasy than before. But why wasn't Joy with Tom? He seemed like a nice, successful kind of guy. He was clearly interested in marrying her. So why did she remain single?

They didn't speak the entire way back to Bee Tree Hill.

Chase pulled into the circle drive and parked the Jeep near the front door. When he turned off the engine, they sat in silence for a heartbeat before they spoke at the same time.

"Who is Tom?"

"Tom is an old friend."

Again, silence.

"How long have you known him?" Chase asked.

She shrugged. "Since I was in high school. We dated on and off, but then the summer you came…" Her words trailed away.

"Did you connect with him after I left?"

Joy's fists rested on her knees and she let out a sigh. "I would rather not discuss it."

She opened the door and reached into the back to grab a couple gallons of paint, and then went into the mansion.

Chase sat in the Jeep for another minute wishing he

could turn back the clock and do everything differently. He wanted to ask Joy if Tom was the father of her twins, but he suspected he already knew the truth.

They looked just like the overly friendly lawyer.

Chapter Four

❧

Early morning sunshine streamed through the multi-paned window of Joy's small sitting room. It connected to the master bedroom and served as her private office, as well as a place for her morning devotions. The window was cracked just enough for her to feel the fresh air and hear the birds singing in the basswood trees just beyond the mansion. In July, they would bloom and their fragrance would fill the air with the sweetest perfume. The trees also attracted honeybees, which was how the estate had been named.

But her mind wasn't on the honeybees, or even the beautiful morning. From her vantage point, she had a view of the carriage house, distracting her and causing her to think about Chase.

The previous afternoon, when they'd returned from the hardware store, they had gone their separate ways. He had started to fix some of the minor, more bother-some issues around the house, and she had gone into the girls' room to start clearing out the furniture for Chase to paint the walls. The boys had followed Chase around for the remainder of the day, and though she had tried to call them away from him several times, he'd insisted that he didn't mind. Instead of grow impatient, he had taught them how to use a hammer and screwdriver, showed them how to replace a hinge and water faucet and even did a little math with them using his measuring tape.

And they didn't even complain about adding when they were on summer break.

While Chase had put blue painters tape around the trim in the girls' room, and Mrs. Thompson had entertained the girls with some gardening, Joy had begun working on the grants and fund-raising efforts to buy Bee Tree Hill. She hadn't gotten far, though, since the girls' room was close to her office and she could hear Chase talking with the boys. They hung on his every word and told him things they'd never told her. She'd tried not to eavesdrop, but she couldn't help it. She'd learned things about the boys' past that made her want to weep for them—but throughout the conversation, Chase had been a pillar of support for the boys, never pressuring them to talk, or making them feel unimportant.

Now, as she sat in her office, researching possible grants online, her gaze drifted to the window, searching for a glimpse of the man who still made her heart gallop, despite her best efforts.

"How about a cup of coffee and a friendly face?" Mrs. Thompson asked, entering the room with two steaming mugs.

The smell of freshly-brewed coffee made Joy turn her attention away from the window. "Always," she said with a smile.

Mrs. Thompson handed Joy one cup and took a seat on the lounge chair near Joy's desk. She settled back and put her feet on the ottoman, a satisfied smile touching her lips just before she took a sip of the coffee. "The first sip is my favorite."

Joy leaned back in her chair and did the same. "You make the best coffee."

Mrs. Thompson held her cup between her two palms and studied Joy. "When are you going to tell him?"

With a sigh, Joy set her cup on her desk and crossed her arms and legs, not ready to face this topic.

"When you became pregnant," Mrs. Thompson said, "Morgan wanted you to call Chase—"

"And I did—he just didn't answer."

"If you remember correctly, Morgan said he'd find a number that would work, but you said you weren't ready and made us promise not to tell him."

"You know how devastated I was when Chase left."

"Yes." Mrs. Thompson took another sip of coffee. "And that's why we didn't pressure you to say anything until after the girls were born. But at that time, you were just trying to keep yourself afloat and finish college."

"That wasn't a good time to tell him, either." Indignation rose in Joy's chest. "I had as much as I could handle just surviving. I didn't need the added emotional stress of telling Chase about the girls." Or worrying that he might take them from her.

"And when you finally had a handle on being a single mom and you finished college," she patted Joy's knee, "—which I'm so proud of you for—then you were busy trying to find a job."

"I couldn't handle telling Chase when I was dealing with everything else."

"But then you found a job," Mrs. Thompson continued, "and I told you it was time to tell Chase, but then you learned about the boys and decided to start fostering them."

"And I couldn't have done it without you and Uncle Morgan."

"We were happy to help," she said, "but, honey, it's time to tell Chase."

Joy shook her head. "Not now, not when we've just learned that we might be homeless."

Leaning forward, Mrs. Thompson leveled her gaze on Joy. "Life will never be perfect enough to tell Chase the truth. Something will always come up. We're either in a crisis, just past a crisis or about to enter one. If you wait too long, and he learns the truth some other way, it will just cause more pain."

Lifting her mug off the desk, Joy couldn't deny Mrs. Thompson's wisdom. When was the last time her life was uncomplicated? When might everything be perfect enough for her to tell Chase he was a father?

Joy lowered her cup to her lap. The brown liquid was more hazelnut creamer than coffee. She was quiet for a moment as she took stock of her real fear. "What if he tried to take them?"

"I know that's the real reason you haven't told him." Mrs. Thompson set her coffee on the desk and scooted forward to place her hands on Joy's knees. "But you can't let that keep you from telling him the truth. I know he left, and I know he hurt you, but I also know that those two baby girls need to know who their daddy is—and he needs to know them." She put one hand under Joy's chin and tilted her face up. "God's got this, honey. He's not surprised by any of it. He's not surprised that Chase is back, or that he came to sell the estate or that you're afraid to say something."

"But how do I know it will come out okay in the end?"

"You don't. All you can hope is that God will use this for your good and His glory, no matter how things turn out."

Joy took a deep breath and tried to nod. She realized Mrs. Thompson spoke the truth—she just had a hard time believing it. "What if—" She paused, almost more afraid of the alternative thought that had plagued her all these years. "What if he doesn't want anything to do with them?"

"Kind of like your daddy didn't want you?" She spoke gently, but the words dug into Joy like a knife.

She couldn't even respond.

"I wish I could promise you that Chase will do the right thing—but I can't. I also wish I could promise you that he'll be a good daddy—but I can't. What I can promise you is that God will always be the Father you and those girls need—and, God willing, I'll be here to help as much as I can."

Joy set her coffee on the desk and leaned into Mrs. Thompson's embrace. The older woman was as dear to Joy as a real mother—something Joy had not had since she was nine years old.

"I love you," Joy said to her surrogate mama. "I'm so happy you're a part of my life."

"I love you, too, honey." Mrs. Thompson sat back and took her coffee again. "And I'll be praying for you and Chase and those children." She winked and nodded. "You'll see—God has a plan and everything will turn out exactly how He wants it to turn out."

Joy clung to Mrs. Thompson's confidence, even though she didn't have any herself. Life had taught her to expect and prepare for the worst, and though she hated that about herself, she didn't know how to change.

She would continue to fight for her children—and she would do what was best for them, even if what was best was also what was hardest.

"You know what we should build?" Ryan asked with his eyes big and bright.

"What?" Chase set the first board against the trunk of

the tree and held it in place until he could pound a nail through the wood.

"A skylight, so we can look out at the stars. Then, we can have a sleepover in the fort to watch them."

"You can't watch the stars while you sleep, silly," Jordan said, shaking his head.

"No!" Ryan rolled his eyes. "We'll watch the stars until we fall asleep."

Kodi cheered at the idea, but Chase simply nodded, as if he was considering the request. "We'll have to see. I'm not sure I can build such a fancy fort."

"You can build anything," Kodi said with awe in his voice.

Chase grinned and started to hammer the nail into place. "Could you fill my tool belt with a few more nails, Jordan?"

Jordan jumped to help and pulled several nails out of a box, then he put them in the tool belt around Chase's waist.

The warm June weather was as perfect as it could get without the addition of mosquitoes or other pesky bugs. Those would come later in the summer, if Chase's memory was correct. For now, the bright blue skies, warm breezes and occasional thunderstorms made this his favorite month of the year.

"We'll put a few boards on the tree for a ladder and then we'll start on the platform," Chase explained to the boys. "Hopefully we can get a good start on that before suppertime."

"Are you going to eat with us again?" Ryan asked. "I heard Mama tell Mrs. Thompson it was *awkward* to have you eat with us and she wished you didn't."

Chase paused as he put another nail in place. Joy didn't want him eating with her and the children? He tried not to feel offended or embarrassed by the revelation, but he shouldn't be surprised.

"Ryan!" Jordan said. "That's not nice."

Ryan just shrugged. "I didn't say it—she did."

Jordan put his hand on Chase's shoulder. "I want you there." He smiled. "I like you."

"So do I," said Ryan, defensively.

"And me," agreed Kodi.

"I like you guys, too." Chase hammered the second nail in place and then tried to wiggle the first board. It didn't budge. "But if your mom doesn't want me eating with you, then I should probably start eating in the carriage house."

"No!" the boys cried in protest.

"See?" Jordan pushed Ryan with his shoulder, a frown on his face.

"It'll be okay," Chase tried to assure him, taking another board and placing it above the first. "I'll still see you all the time." His phone started to vibrate in his back pocket. He'd turned the ringer off, because it felt like too much of an intrusion into this idyllic place. "I need to take this call," he said to the boys. "Ryan, do you want to try to nail the next board into place like I just did?"

"Sure!" Ryan grabbed the hammer from Chase and set to work.

Chase pulled the phone from his pocket and tried not to cringe. It was his dad.

Tapping the green icon, he took a steadying breath. "Hello."

"I have someone interested in the property."

"Hi, Dad."

"He's in Singapore right now, but he will be back later this summer." Dad's voice was impatient, as usual. "I need you to get me as much information about the property as possible, and as soon as possible. I need the exact acreage of the estate, the dimensions of the house, including each room, and an appraisal of the house, property and artifacts. The buyer wants as many pictures of the riverfront property as possible. Go across the river to the park and take them from there, too."

Chase moved away from the boys so he could speak plainly, while still keeping them in his line of sight. He didn't want them to do anything foolish, like use the saw he'd brought with his other tools—but he also didn't want them hearing what he might say to his dad. No use scaring them about losing Bee Tree Hill, if it wasn't necessary.

"I have someone interested in the property, too," Chase said. It was Joy, but his father didn't need to know that.

"Perfect. A bidding war would be even better."

A bidding war? Joy had no hope of winning a bidding war.

"When can you get me all the information?" Dad asked in a clipped tone.

"When do you need it?" He had to stall for more time.

"Last week." Dad's voice held no room for small talk.

"I'll see what I can do."

"No. You'll do exactly as I asked and nothing less."

Chase had been at the mansion for three days and had not even called the appraiser yet. He'd been too busy working on projects.

"I'll have everything to you as soon as possible."

"Good." The phone went dead.

Chase pulled it away to make certain his father was no longer on the line and then turned off the device, stuffing it into his pocket in frustration.

"Was that your dad?" Ryan asked, holding the hammer loose in his hand. All three boys watched Chase closely.

"Yes."

"Where does he live?" Kodi asked.

"Far away." But not far enough.

"Our dad lives far away, too," Jordan said.

Ryan frowned. "How do you know?"

"If he lived close, he'd come for us." Jordan stood with his shoulders bent. "Wouldn't he?"

Ryan shrugged. "I don't know." Then he looked at Chase. "Do you know?"

Chase shook his head. He didn't know anything about the boys' birth parents. "I wish I did, buddy." He put his hand on Ryan's shoulder. "Should we get back to work?"

Ryan's face lit up and he nodded. "Did I do a good job?"

The nail Ryan had put into the board had gone in sideways and was bent, but Chase nodded. "It looks great. I'll just add a second one for a little more support."

As Chase pounded in a second nail, Joy appeared at the top of the hill with a man by her side. He wore khaki shorts and a green polo shirt.

Tom Winston.

Chase couldn't hide the displeasure he felt. What did the lawyer want?

They walked down the stone steps to the bottom of the hill while Chase continued to pound the ladder into the tree.

"Boys," Joy called out to Ryan, Jordan and Kodi when they drew closer. "Look who came to visit."

"Tom!" the boys called out to the new arrival, but none of them left Chase's side.

"Hey, guys." Tom had his hands in his pockets, but

now he took one hand out to take off his sunglasses. "What are you building?"

"A tree fort!" Ryan and Jordan answered at the same time.

Chase set down his hammer and wiped his hands on his shorts before extending one hand to Tom. "It's good to see you again." Although, it wasn't.

Tom's handshake was strong and confident. "Same to you."

"Tom's here to mow the lawn," Joy said quickly. "It takes hours."

Chase had already noticed that the lawn was getting tall—but he'd been too busy with other things. "There's no need," he said. "I was planning to do it in the morning."

"No worries." Tom put his sunglasses back on. "I'm here to do it now. You don't need to bother."

"No bother at all." Chase crossed his arms. "It's why I came."

"Is it?" Tom asked. "I thought you were here to sell—"

"Maybe Tom can mow the bottom of the hill and Chase, you can mow the top," Joy said quickly, interrupting him, probably so the boys wouldn't hear what he had to say about selling the estate. "It takes a couple hours to do each—there are several acres to mow, after all."

"I'll start and see how far I get before nightfall," Tom said. "I can always come back tomorrow after work and finish—" he looked at the tree fort "—since Chase has other things to worry about."

In Chase's opinion, the tree fort was more important than the lawn, but the way Tom said it suggested that Chase was playing when there was work to do.

"Why don't you join us for supper, Tom?" Joy asked,

clearly changing the subject. "Mrs. Thompson is making Chinese food tonight—egg rolls and chicken lo mein."

Ryan cheered at the news.

"I'd be happy to join you," Tom said with a big grin.

Given the information the boys had shared earlier, Chase had planned to dine alone that evening—but now that he knew Tom was going to be there, he changed his mind. "I love egg rolls," he said.

"Great." Joy put her hands on Ryan's shoulders and eyed up the progress on the tree fort—which wasn't much—but she still smiled. "I can't wait to see what this looks like when you boys are finished."

Ryan lifted his shoulders with pride—and Chase couldn't deny that he also felt a little proud, too.

Maybe they would put a skylight in, after all.

Chapter Five

"When was the last time you used the firepit down by the river?" Chase asked Joy later that evening as he helped Mrs. Thompson clear the table after supper.

Joy looked at Mrs. Thompson, who shrugged.

Memories of the last time she'd sat by the firepit returned unbidden and Joy couldn't meet Chase's gaze. The two of them had lit a fire, popped popcorn over the flames and watched the annual fireworks together. "I suppose it's been four years now," she said.

Tom also stood and started to help clear plates, while the children finished drinking their milk.

"What do you think about lighting a fire and making s'mores for dessert?" Chase asked.

"Yay!" the kids all cheered.

"I love s'mores," Kinsley said with a starry-eyed grin.

"I can save the brownies for tomorrow night," Mrs. Thompson offered. "A fire sounds so nice."

"I'll get some firewood in the old wagon," Ryan added. "I know right where it's at by the barn and the old beehives."

"I can help!" Jordan said.

Both boys jumped up before Joy could protest. She

had things to do this evening. She had found half a dozen grants and she had hours of work ahead of her—not to mention some correspondence with the boys' social worker. After years of working with the boys' birth mother, and countless classes and counseling sessions to teach her the skills she'd need to properly care for them, a final court date had been set to evaluate her progress. Though Joy was rooting for their birth mother, and prayed for her daily, she was sad to think of the boys leaving them. But that was part of her agreement as a foster mom. She was available for as long as needed, and willing to do whatever was best for Ryan, Jordan and Kodi.

An email had come through that morning from the social worker, but Joy had not had time to read it—and it looked like she wouldn't get to it for several more hours.

"Mind if I join you?" Tom asked Joy. "I don't like s'mores—but I enjoy the company."

"Of course you're welcome to join us," Joy said. S'mores were one of her favorite treats—did Chase remember?

"Do you have all the ingredients?" Chase asked Mrs. Thompson. "Or should I run up to the store?"

"We should have everything here." Mrs. Thompson went to the pantry at the end of the servants' stairs. She opened the beadboard doors and pushed a few things around. "I was right!" she called out in a singsong voice. "I have everything we'll need."

Chase set a dirty plate in the soapy water and glanced at Joy. "Do you mind having a fire?"

"Of course not." How could she say no now that everyone had their hopes up? She took a clean rag and wiped Harper's hands and face.

Chase followed her and picked up Harper's empty cup. "I remember how much you like s'mores."

So he did remember.

"And campfires," he added with a knowing smile, "if I'm not mistaken."

Harper watched Chase closely, still uncertain of the stranger who had been with them almost constantly these past three days.

Joy's cheeks warmed at the campfire memories, though she didn't know why. Nothing had happened with Chase that evening. It had been early in their relationship and he had done nothing more than brush her shoulder with his own.

"I remember making s'mores at camp." Tom interrupted Joy's thoughts as he approached the table to take a few more dishes. "Even as a kid, I didn't like them. They're really sweet."

"Just like Joy," Chase said with a wink.

Mrs. Thompson laughed, but Joy pretended not to hear him.

"Leave the dishes," Chase said to Mrs. Thompson when she returned to the sink.

She protested, but he pulled her away.

"I can't relax when I know the dishes will be waiting for me when I return." She tried to go back to the sink, but Chase shook his head.

"I'll do them when we come back inside," he told her. "Tonight is your night off."

Joy liked the sound of that. Mrs. Thompson worked harder than three women her age. Instead of enjoying retirement as most women were doing, she was taking care of five busy children and a ten-thousand-square-foot house. "I'll help Chase," Joy offered. "Consider the dishes done."

"I couldn't possibly," Mrs. Thompson said.

"Yes, you could." Joy helped Chase lead her away

from the sink. "Don't forget your sweater. It'll probably cool down once the sun sets."

Mrs. Thompson sighed. "Alright." A smile lit her wrinkled face and a twinkle filled her eyes. "I suppose it won't hurt me, just this once." She left the kitchen to retrieve a sweater.

Kinsley climbed out of her booster seat and Harper lifted her hands for Joy to carry her.

"Do the girls need sweaters, too?" Chase asked.

"I was just going to run up and grab them," Joy said, taking Harper into her arms.

"I'll go." He started toward the stairs. "Are they in the dresser?"

"Hanging in their closet." She tried to hide her surprise. Mrs. Thompson helped Joy with the kids all the time, but she'd rarely had anyone else offer.

"Pink for Kinsley and purple for Harper?" he asked.

Joy nodded, even more surprised that he remembered.

"I'll be right back." He took the stairs two at a time and disappeared around the corner.

"Is he always so helpful?" Tom asked dryly, dropping the last of the dirty dishes into the sink.

Joy shrugged. "He's only been here three days."

Tom let his gaze wander to the stairs and he shook his head. "I don't quite trust him. He's too nice."

"Too nice?" Joy asked, swallowing her own misgivings. "He was always helpful the summer he lived here, offering to aid Mr. and Mrs. Thompson whenever he could, reading to Uncle Morgan, who was losing his eyesight…" She let her words trail away, because she remembered how attentive Chase had been to her, as well, offering to bring her to the store, move heavy furniture when she vacuumed, fetch her things when she had her hands full. It was just his way—and it had always made Joy feel noticed and even loved.

Until he left. At first, she had questioned Chase's intentions all along, but over time—and especially now, seeing him again—she realized acts of service was one of his love languages. Whether or not he abandoned her, it didn't negate his care and concern when they were together.

Tom frowned. "He suddenly shows up, four years too late, and he wants to play daddy?"

"Shh." Joy put her finger to her lips and looked pointedly at the girls and Kodi, who was watching them closely.

"Chase wants to be our dad?" A look of pure excitement filled Kodi's bright blue eyes with hope.

"No," Joy said a bit quicker than necessary. "He's just a friend."

"I hope you're right." Tom crossed his arms, displeasure on his handsome face. He leaned against the countertop. "I'd hate to see him hurt you again—and this time, there are five more people he could trample on his way out."

"Please don't," Joy said gently to Tom as she set Harper on her feet. "It's not the time or the place."

Despite her protests, his warning was hitting too close to Joy's own fears.

Tom sighed and pushed away from the counter. "You're right. I think I better leave. I can't sit here and watch him manipulate your feelings again."

His words felt like a slap to her face and she stared at him for a second before she found the ability to answer. "Perhaps you should leave."

He didn't say goodbye, but simply left the kitchen through the back door.

The kids watched him leave, a bit wide-eyed.

What he said hurt—especially because Joy feared he was right. Was she letting Chase back into her heart? Would he hurt her again?

This time, she had the children to worry about. She couldn't let Chase hurt them.

"I think I'm ready," Mrs. Thompson said, returning to the kitchen. If she noticed Tom had left, she didn't say anything. She looked several years younger as she eagerly placed the ingredients for s'mores, along with a book of matches, a washcloth to clean sticky hands and a small bucket of soapy water in a wicker basket. "I'll take Kodi down to the firepit and make sure the other boys haven't tried to start the fire yet."

As she and Kodi left, the top step creaked and a couple moments later, Chase reappeared with the sweaters.

"What happened to Tom?" he asked.

"He needed to leave."

Chase didn't say anything, but his smile said enough.

While he helped Kinsley put on her sweater, Joy helped Harper, and she couldn't stop herself from thinking about Tom's warning. Did Chase have ulterior motives?

"Are we ready?" Chase asked.

"Yes!" Kinsley ran to the door and pulled it open. "I want s'mores!"

"Reminds me of her mother." Chase grinned as he held the door open. "Ladies first."

They left the house and took the stone steps to the bottom of the hill.

Everything the light touched looked like gold in the setting sunshine. White trellises with climbing vines adorned the north end of the property, while a green gazebo sat perched on a little rise near the river. A white picket fence encircled the carriage house yard and a long chain-link fence ran the length of the north side of the property, which bordered a pond and community park.

Kinsley and Chase moved just slightly ahead, with Kinsley talking as fast as her little mouth could move. "I like s'mores," she said to Chase, "but I also like ice cream."

"I like ice cream, too," Chase agreed. "Chocolate is my favorite."

Kinsley looked up at him and grinned. "I like chocolate, too."

Their side profiles were so similar, Joy caught her breath.

How much longer could she keep her secret? Already, Chase had been at Bee Tree Hill long enough that it would be awkward to suddenly bring it up. She couldn't just approach him with the information. Maybe it would come up naturally.

The firepit was actually a fireplace with a chimney built on a little stone pier along the banks of the Mississippi. The pier was as old as the mansion itself. Joy liked to imagine the Asher family spending time around the fireplace since the 1890s. A stone bench lined the pier, and steps alongside it went right into the water. Joy tried to avoid bringing the kids near the water at all costs, and had given the boys strict instructions when they played outside alone. The girls were never allowed outside by themselves, and a part of her was hesitant to even let them know about the pier. She'd have to be adamant with them about staying away from the water again.

Mrs. Thompson and the boys met them at the pier and Chase ruffled Kodi's hair.

"I'll show you how to start a fire," he told the boys,

motioning for them to come close to him near the fireplace.

Joy groaned. "The last thing they need is to learn how to start a fire."

Chase only smiled at her mothering and showed them how to lay the kindling inside the fireplace. With a strike of the match, he set the flame to the dry leaves and sticks and then fanned the flame to life. As he worked, the boys squatted next to him, eagerly listening, and when he said it was time to lay more sticks of wood on the fire, they did—very carefully.

"Girls," Joy said to Harper and Kinsley, "stay back from the ledge."

"What we need are some long sticks," Chase told the boys next. "We'll use those to roast the marshmallows."

"I get long sticks!" Kinsley said.

"I can, too." Jordan raised his hand.

The boys ran off with Kinsley following close behind.

"Boys," Joy said, "watch Kinsley closely and don't leave my eyesight."

"Okay."

Joy took a seat on the bench and Harper stood next to her, leaning against Joy's knee as she watched her siblings looking for the perfect sticks.

"Have you given any thought to your fund-raising efforts?" Chase asked Joy.

Any thought? It was all she thought about. "I have."

"It's actually one of the reasons I wanted to gather everyone together tonight," he said as he stood by the fireplace, his eyes on the kids.

For some reason, Joy's heartbeat sped. Did Chase have important news about the sale of Bee Tree Hill? "What did you want to discuss?" she asked.

"I had an idea for a fund-raiser." Chase stood with a

wide stance, his arms crossed. Behind him, the Mississippi was high and the current was strong. It wasn't very wide so close to the headwaters, but it was fast.

"What did you have in mind?" Mrs. Thompson asked. She sat next to Joy and motioned for Harper to climb into her lap.

"For years, people in this community have been curious about this property." Chase's eyes shone with his idea. "Why don't we have an event to honor the family's legacy and offer tours of the house? We could have volunteers dress up in period clothing to give the tours. We could also have an ice-cream-and-lemonade social on the lawn and offer games that were popular in the 1890s when the house was built."

Joy's heart sped up for an entirely different reason. "It's a wonderful idea. We could ask the auto club to bring some of the old Model T cars and offer rides and I could ask Margie at the historical society to help with the games." Her mind raced with ideas. "We'll need time to plan and advertise, but I think we could hold it the last weekend in July." Just before their eviction. Maybe, if they were successful with the fund-raiser, grants and other income sources, they wouldn't be evicted, after all.

The children returned with several long sticks—and a few short ones from Kinsley—and Chase showed them how to sharpen the tips with his pocket knife so the marshmallow would slip on easily.

Together, they helped the children roast their marshmallows while Mrs. Thompson prepared the chocolate and graham crackers.

Joy couldn't help but glance at Chase while he laughed with the boys.

When he looked up at her, he smiled, and she remembered all the reasons she had fallen in love with him. He was confident, smart, kind and one of the most generous people she'd ever met—thankfully she also knew his faults, because if she didn't, she might find herself falling for him all over again.

Chase couldn't take his eyes off Joy as the fire cracked and sizzled. She had to be the prettiest mom he'd ever seen—but, she was more than pretty. She was amazingly patient with the kids, though she parented with authority gained out of respect.

After the s'mores were eaten, they had sung a few camp songs, and told some stories. As the first stars sparkled in the growing darkness, Joy sighed. "It's time for bed."

The kids started to complain, and Chase couldn't deny that he was also disappointed.

"We have a busy day tomorrow," she said. "We need to start making plans for the Bee Tree Hill Festival."

Harper lay in Joy's arms, almost asleep. Her plump cheeks were pink from the heat of the fire and she had chocolate around her little mouth. She still watched him cautiously, but at least she didn't run away from him anymore.

When Joy stood, Harper snuggled into her shoulder.

Kinsley also yawned as she sat on the bench next to Chase, her sticky hand on his leg. Mrs. Thompson had wiped her fingers with her washcloth, but somehow she'd made them sticky again.

"Would you like me to carry you to the house?" he asked her.

She nodded and lifted her arms for him to pick her up. He did, and was surprised at how light she felt.

"Should we put out the fire?" Ryan asked.

"Just dump the bucket of water on the coals," Chase

told him. He stood with Kinsley in his arms and watched Ryan do as he said while Mrs. Thompson walked Jordan and Kodi toward the house.

Joy also stood and watched Ryan.

"Thanks for the s'mores," Ryan said to Chase after he was done. "I never made them over a real campfire before."

"How'd you make them?" Chase asked the boy.

They started toward the house and Ryan put his hands in his pockets like a grown-up. "A foster home we lived in had one of those fake campfire machines to make them around the table." He shrugged. "I like them better over a real fire."

"Me, too," Chase agreed.

"Why don't you run ahead to Mrs. Thompson?" Joy asked him. "Wash up and then get your pajamas on. I'll be in to pray for you as soon as I get the girls in bed."

Ryan did as she instructed and took off across the lawn. At least a dozen yard lights lit up the lower part of the property.

Kinsley nestled her head into Chase's shoulder and was soon breathing deeply. He rested his hand against her back, marveling at the way she trusted him to carry her safely inside.

"Thank you," Joy said to him, "for being patient with the boys."

"They're great kids." He wanted to ask about their birth parents, but didn't know how much he could ask—or how much she could tell him. "How long have they been in the foster system?"

"Six years. Ryan was only two when they were removed from their birth mother's home. Jordan was one and Kodi was just born." She rubbed Harper's back as she walked. The little girl had her thumb in her mouth and her eyes were closed. "The county became aware of the neglect when their mother was in the hospital delivering Kodi. Apparently, Ryan and Jordan were at home alone when she was brought in."

"At the ages of two and one?" Chase could hardly believe his ears.

"It was worse than just being alone." She sighed. "When the county got to their home, the living conditions were horrendous and the boys had bruises from the mom's boyfriend. So they were put into an emergency foster home, and then moved from place to place. Their mother has been in and out of rehab, and she's had custody periodically over the years, but she has relapsed every time. Two years ago, the county approached me and asked if I'd offer a more permanent foster home for them while their mom goes through treatment one more time."

"I can't even imagine." Chase struggled with his father, but at least he'd never been afraid of losing his home or being taken care of.

"I want, more than anything, to give those boys a real home—one they never have to leave, unless they want to go."

Chase wished he could promise her that she wouldn't have to move, but he couldn't. "I will do whatever I can to help."

"I know—and I'm thankful." One of the yard lights lit up her face, making her eyes shine.

They walked up the hill and into the house through the kitchen door.

Chase followed Joy up the servants' stairs to the girls' bedroom, near the top of the steps. She turned on a lamp and laid Harper on one of the toddler beds. "You can lay Kinsley down and I'll get their pajamas."

Chase did as she instructed and the little girl curled

into a ball. They were so small and delicate. Again, he wondered about their father. Watching Tom tonight, he had become convinced that his first guess was wrong. There was very little interaction between Tom and the girls. Wouldn't he be more interested in them if they were his daughters?

Joy turned back from the dresser with two pairs of footie pajamas and Night Time Pull-Ups.

"Do you need help?" he asked.

She lifted her eyebrows. "Do you really want to help?"

He nodded. "I don't know much about kids, but I learn quickly."

"Alright." She looked skeptical, but handed him a set of pajamas and a Pull-Up.

They worked side by side, though Joy was much more adept than him. Kinsley was no help, since she stayed asleep through the whole event.

Finally, when Joy finished with Harper, and tucked her into her little bed, she came to help Chase.

"It's easier to put her legs into the pajamas first," she said with a smile in her voice. "Then put in her arms and zip it up."

Chase stepped aside and watched.

When she was done, she put Kinsley under her covers, and then laid her hand on the little girl's forehead and said a prayer. "May God bless and keep you, may God's face shine on you, may God be kind to you and give you peace." She leaned down and kissed Kinsley's forehead, then she went back to Harper and said the same blessing.

She tilted her head toward the door. Chase walked across the room and exited. She followed, flipping off the lamp and closing the door.

Down the hall, the boys were laughing.

"They have a lot of energy," she said with a smile.

Chase and Joy stood just outside the girls' bedroom door in the dark hallway.

"You amaze me," he said without thinking.

She met his gaze. "I'm only doing what God gives me the strength to do."

"That's what is amazing. Most people wouldn't have the ability to do any of this."

"I can't take the credit."

"You should, because you deserve it."

She shifted her weight uncomfortably and didn't meet his gaze. "Good night, Chase."

"Can I say good-night to the boys?"

She nodded and he followed her down the hall to the boys' room. Mrs. Thompson had already helped them get into their pajamas and they were lying in their beds. The room was long and had three separate beds, as well as three dressers and three desks. The walls were papered in a blue pattern and the carpet was white. Even though it was occupied by the boys, it was surprisingly tidy. Joy and Mrs. Thompson did a great job keeping the place clean.

"Ready for your blessing?" Joy asked.

The boys said yes all at once, so Joy went to each bed and did exactly as she had done for the girls. She laid her hand on their foreheads and prayed. Each of the boys closed their eyes and a happy little smile turned up their lips.

"They never let me forget their prayer," Joy said and then kissed Ryan's forehead.

"Who prays for you?" Chase asked her.

Joy's face went still for a brief second and then she looked back at Ryan, pushing his hair off his face. "Mrs. Thompson prays for me."

"I pray for you, too, Mama," Ryan said, snuggling into his pillow.

"Good night," she whispered to him.

"Good night, boys," Chase added.

The boys called back their good-nights and then he and Joy left the room. When she closed the bedroom door, he found himself in the hallway again with her. Alone.

"I had a good time tonight, Joy." So many good memories had returned to him while they'd sat on the pier. "Thank you for letting me be part of your life."

"How long will you be here this time?" she asked, not looking at his face.

"For as long as it takes to sell the place, I suppose."

"And then what?"

"Then—" He paused. He supposed he'd return to Seattle, though the thought didn't hold as much appeal as it should. Bee Tree Hill had a way of pulling him in and making him feel at peace. Returning to Seattle felt like he was leaving home. "I'll take things a day at a time. But I'll do whatever I can to help. When I get back to the carriage house, I'll work on some posters for the festival."

It wasn't much, but it was something.

Chapter Six

There were so many things Joy needed to do three nights after the campfire, but she found herself in the music room with an album Mrs. Thompson had put together from the girls' first year of life.

The kids were in bed, Mrs. Thompson was in her room reading and Joy didn't have the heart to write another grant application tonight. She'd already done two and her mind was exhausted.

After the house quieted, she had come downstairs to turn off the lights and caught sight of the scrapbook. As she sat on one of the ornate couches near the marble fireplace, she relived that first uncertain year through pictures. A single lamp was the only source of light in the room, but it was all she needed.

Intermingled with the delight and wonder in the pictures and in the memories, she remembered the fear, pain and heartache. But wasn't that what life was? A mixture of joy and sorrow?

A picture of Harper and Kinsley, bundled in swaddling blankets that said "I received my first hug at the Timber Falls Hospital," snuggled against one another on the hospital bed, made Joy smile. She ran her finger over the glossy page and could hardly believe it had been three years since they had joined her life.

If she was honest with herself, she knew why she'd pulled out the scrapbook. She had to tell Chase the truth, and she wanted him to have a glimpse of what he had missed these past three years. He had every right to know he was a father—and every right to the memories she had—even if he had abandoned her.

But she would have to reassure him that she didn't want or expect anything from him. He wasn't obligated to provide for them—on the contrary, the less the Asher family had to do with her girls, the better.

The steps into the music room creaked and Joy looked up quickly.

Chase stood on the second step, a piece of paper in his hand. "Mrs. Thompson let me in at the kitchen door."

Joy's heart sped up at the sight of him and her cheeks grew warm. Even though she'd resolved to tell him the truth, nerves got the better of her. What if she told him and he wanted to fight for custody? What if his father stepped in and demanded his rights?

"I finally finished the poster." He walked down the rest of the steps into the music room, his dark hair brushing his forehead, his button-down shirt rolled at the sleeves and his loose khaki pants rolled at the ankles. He wore Birkenstock sandals and looked like he should be lounging on a beach somewhere.

Joy didn't stand, but waited for him to join her at the couch. She closed the scrapbook and set it beside her, not wanting him to see what she'd been looking at until after she'd told him the news—if she found the courage.

He stood in front of her and held out the poster.

Taking it, she positioned it to get the best light from the lamp—and stared. In the center was a penciled rendering of Bee Tree Hill House and in elegant vintage script he'd filled in all the information about the festival, including the reason behind the event. It said that all proceeds would go to the Gordon family housing fund.

"This is amazing, Chase." She pulled it closer and looked at the details of the drawing. "Where did you get the picture of the mansion?"

"I drew it."

She looked up at him, her surprise too strong to hide. "You can draw?"

He shrugged and sat beside her. "I always liked to draw, but when my father forced me to take a master's class in high school, it became a chore instead of a hobby." He studied the picture with her. "But ever since returning to Bee Tree Hill, I've wanted to draw the house."

"It's incredible." She shook her head. "This should be framed and hung over the mantel."

"It's not that nice." He laughed and took the poster back from her. "I just did a rough drawing for the poster. Do you think it'll work?"

She couldn't take her eyes off the picture. It was an amazing likeness and held all the charm she loved about Bee Tree Hill. "It's perfect."

"I thought I could take it to the print shop and have some copies made tomorrow," Chase said, "and then the boys and I can deliver them around town—if it's okay with you."

"They'd like that."

"Do you think they'd like to ride in the Jeep?"

"Of course." She smiled. "Just make sure you have the top down."

"Maybe I'll take them to the Dairy Dream for some ice cream treats afterward." He watched her carefully, as if he expected her to say that he'd gone too far—but he hadn't. She appreciated that he wanted to spend time with the boys. They needed it—and maybe Chase needed them, too.

"I'll send money along for them," she offered.

He shook his head. "It's my treat."

Joy nodded, knowing it didn't pay to debate with him. "Thank you," she said instead, growing nervous again about what she needed to tell him. "They like spending time with you. It means a lot to them." She hoped he realized how much. "But please don't tell them you're bringing them until you actually do. If you make a promise that you can't keep, it will only hurt them."

He worked his jaw for a second. "I wouldn't do that to them, Joy."

He'd only do that to her, then? She wanted to voice her thoughts, but knew nothing good could come from them. "I need to protect them," she said instead. "In a few weeks, their birth mother will make a court appearance and the judge will make a final decision about her rights. I received an email from their social worker and it doesn't look good for their mother. She's missed several appointments, shown little improvement in the past six months and is currently with a man who has several felonies."

His face filled with anger and then disappointment. "What will happen to them then? Is their father in the picture?"

She shook her head. "Their mom did not name their fathers." And she wouldn't—because Joy suspected that the birth mom didn't know who to name. "So if her rights are taken away, the boys will become—"

"Orphans."

"Yes." Her heart broke just thinking about the implications.

"Will you try to adopt them?" he asked.

She looked down at her empty hands. "I don't know if the judge would allow me to adopt them—a single mom with questionable housing." She wouldn't wallow in what-ifs. If God wanted her to adopt those boys, He'd find a way. "I just want to make sure you completely understand how important it is for you to keep your word."

The lamplight softened his features. "I know I haven't done anything to deserve it, but I'm asking you to trust me—with the boys, and with—" He paused and she held her breath. "With everything else."

It was the moment she'd been waiting for—her pounding heart told her so. He asked her to trust him...with everything. Was it time to trust him with the whole truth?

Chase rose from the couch and picked up the poster. "I'll check with you in the morning to see if the boys are still free to go."

He started to walk away from her and all she could do was watch him leave. He was extending an invitation to take a risk on him again, and everything inside her head shouted at her not to take the risk. But it was the cry of her heart that made the loudest noise and it pleaded with her to give him another chance. Not a chance at love— but at believing he was a good man, just as she'd once believed—that he could also be a good father.

The grandfather clock chimed ten times as he took the first step out of the music room.

Joy rose on shaking legs, her stomach rolling, her head spinning and her eyes already filling with tears.

"Chase," she called out to him. "Wait."

He turned, his blue eyes full of a deep sorrow, and in that moment, she wanted to believe that he was remorseful, that leaving hurt him as much as it had hurt her.

With one foot on the bottom step and one hand on the railing, Chase waited.

"I—I have something to tell you." She didn't think her legs would hold her up for much longer, but she forced herself to stand. She was afraid she might be sick and knew her face revealed the myriad of emotions spiraling through her, because Chase frowned and walked across the room.

"What's wrong?" he asked.

She put her hand over her stomach on instinct, trying to calm the turmoil inside her. "Can we sit?"

He nodded and put his hand on her elbow to help her over to the couch.

"You're scaring me," he said.

"I—I don't want to scare you." Though what she had to say might terrify him. She sat and faced him, their knees grazing each other. She took a steadying breath, but it shuddered through her body. "There's something you need to know and I can't put it off any longer."

He set the poster on the coffee table again, giving his full attention to Joy. "Is it about Bee Tree Hill? Mrs. Thompson?" His face filled with concern. "It's not about one of the girls, is it?"

"No—well." She paused. She'd thought about this conversation a hundred times over the past four years, and had imagined dozens of scenarios. But now, when it mattered most, she was at a loss.

She met Chase's gaze and knew it would not come out pretty—but it had to be said.

"Harper and Kinsley are your daughters."

Chase stared at Joy; the words she'd just said hung in the air between them as if she had set them there and it was his job to reach out and take them. But he didn't know how.

He was a father?

A father?

He stood, the truth of her statement hitting him like a jump in the cold waters of the Mississippi. It took his breath away for a second, and he was afraid he might drown with the implications—but then, slowly, as if his body was adjusting, and he was coming up for that first burst of air, his heart started to calm. Images of Kinsley and Harper came to his mind and he couldn't deny what she said. They had Joy's eyes, and her smile, but there were other subtleties about them that reminded him of his own childhood pictures.

His chest started to expand with the truth of Joy's words. The girls were his—his and Joy's. He was their daddy.

"I'm a father?"

She sat, staring up at him, her brown eyes filled with unshed tears, and suddenly, it didn't matter how the news affected him. All he could think about was what she had gone through these past four years, alone, afraid and re-jected.

He sat again and wanted to take her hands into his, but he knew she'd pull away.

"Joy, I'm sorry—sorry I—" But then he paused. He was sorry for leaving her, but how could he be sorry for abandoning his daughters when he didn't know they ex-isted? "Why didn't you tell me?" he asked.

"I tried—for several weeks—but you didn't answer my calls or emails."

Chase shook his head, trying to remember that far back. "I never heard a word from you after I left Bee Tree

Hill. I thought you'd never want to speak to me again."
He would remember if she had tried to contact him.

"I did call—and I sent several emails, too." The lines
around her mouth had deepened and her eyes were full
of so much pain, he could hardly look at her, knowing
he was the cause of her heartache.

He had been such a coward back then, afraid to say
no to his father—but how much had changed? Wasn't he
here at Bee Tree Hill, doing his father's bidding, because
he was afraid to tell him no now?

"Something happened to your messages," he said. "I
didn't receive any of them." His father had sent him to
Europe almost as soon as they had left Bee Tree Hill.
He'd been without a cell phone or email for a month
and a half before returning to the States to go to UCLA.
His father had supplied him with a new phone, and his
email account had become deactivated, so he started a
new one. Had his dad orchestrated all that? Or had it
been an accident?

"But what about later?" He studied her face and she
dropped her gaze to look at her hands. "You've had four
years to tell me about the girls. Mrs. Thompson and Uncle
Morgan contacted me several times about other things—
why didn't you get my number then?" He frowned. "Why
didn't they tell me?"

Joy stood and walked to a lamp. She switched it on,
offering more light—and that was when he saw the book
she'd been looking at when he walked into the room.

Chase picked it up and stared at the front cover. It
was a picture of Joy sitting on a hospital bed, holding
both girls, a beautiful smile on her face. He'd seen other
pictures like it of his friends on Facebook, but usually
the new dad was standing behind the glowing mom—a
first family photo.

Except, in this photo, there was no dad. Chase was missing—and he had no one to blame but himself.

He could never get that moment back. It was gone forever.

Joy didn't answer his previous question as Chase opened the book and found dozens of other photos of her and the girls—and in every single one, there was something missing—him. He wasn't there to hear their first words, see their first smiles, give them their first baths or watch them take their first steps.

"After I learned I was expecting twins, I became scared," Joy said quietly as she walked to the couch and took a seat next to him again. "Scared that if you knew the truth, you'd take the girls."

Her words felt like a jab to the gut. "I'd never take the girls from you, Joy."

"Maybe not," she swallowed hard, "but your father might."

She was right. His father was unpredictable and ruthless. If he knew about Kinsley and Harper, he might either reject them—or try to take them away from Joy completely.

"I would never let him take the girls from you, either." He set the photo book on the poster and faced her again.

The skepticism on her face was well-founded.

"I'm sorry," he said, "for everything. I know I can never make this up to you—and I don't deserve anything from you or the girls—but if you'll let me try, I'd like to be a part of their lives."

She was quiet for a long time. The grandfather clock ticked in the hall, a branch rubbed against a window and the house creaked with age.

"I don't want anything from you," she finally said. "But I also don't want to keep the girls from you, either." She looked up and met his gaze. "I know all too well what it's like to live without a father—and that's something I promised myself I'd never let happen to my own children."

Yet here she was—and at no fault of her own.

"But, Chase." She leaned forward, a tear slipping down her cheek, her voice pleading. "Please, *please* don't break their hearts. I've learned how to live with heartache—but I could not watch you hurt them." She wiped at the tear, impatiently, her voice growing stronger. "If you plan to walk away, then do it now, before they know who you are—before you can hurt them."

Chase swallowed the rush of emotions. "I don't want to walk away." He didn't want to walk away the last time, either. He had wanted to marry Joy and spend the rest of his life with her—it had been fear, and nothing else, that had pulled him away. But he wouldn't let that happen again. "I'm here—for as long as you'll let me be here." Emotions clogged his throat. "I would never hurt those girls." The very thought of anyone hurting them filled him with an entirely new feeling—one that was fierce and swift and instinctual.

He was their dad. He was supposed to be their protector, comforter and champion.

But what if he failed them? On the heels of his desire to protect and shelter the girls was a deep-seated fear that he'd not succeed, that he'd be like his own father—that he'd somehow hurt them, even if he didn't want to. This feeling was even more powerful than the first—because there was so much at stake.

Anxiety filled his chest.

Joy laid her hand over his. It was cool and soft, and brought him out of his chaotic thoughts. "This is a lot of information to take in," she said gently. "Your entire life just changed in a matter of seconds. I understand if you need to take some time to process." She slipped her hand into his and met his gaze with her steady brown eyes. "And I'll understand if it's too much. I really will."

It had taken Chase most of his life to know what he wanted—and he was still uncertain about some things—but he knew, without a doubt in his mind, that he wanted to be a father to those girls. "It isn't too much." He turned his hand over, so their palms were facing each other. It was the first time they'd touched in years, and her skin against his still had the same effect it had before. It filled him with pleasure and longing—but this time, it was more than just a physical desire he felt for her—he longed to make Joy happy again, to relieve her burdens and give her something to smile about. He might never reclaim her heart, but he could reclaim her respect and trust, and if that's all she was willing to give, it would have to be enough. "I will do everything in my power to care for you and the girls. I promise."

Joy slowly pulled her hand away from his and stood. She lifted the photo book off the coffee table and looked at it for a heartbeat before she handed it to him.

He took it, knowing that with it, he was also taking a piece of her trust again. She was offering him a chance to be a dad.

She turned and left the music room, without glancing back.

And in that moment, Chase knew what he could do for Joy. He'd call his dad and tell him he wanted to keep Bee Tree Hill in the family.

Chapter Seven

Morning dew hung on the blades of grass as Chase walked toward the stone pier early the next morning, a cup of steaming coffee in hand. He wore his Birkenstocks and the wet grass made his toes cold, but he hardly noticed. Ever since the night they had taken the kids down to the pier, Chase had gone there each morning to meet the new day and spend quiet time in prayer. His summer with Uncle Morgan and the Thompsons had left an indelible mark on his heart. When he had returned to UCLA, he'd started to attend a Bible study and had given his life to Christ. He had become a new man.

He passed the tree fort and smiled. They'd made more progress in the past few days, but not as much as he'd like. He had spent most of yesterday on the phone with contractors, appraisers and Realtors. He'd scheduled several appointments over the coming week and knew it would be even harder to find the time to help the boys—but he would. He'd made a promise to them and he planned to keep it, no matter the cost.

The rumble of a train sounded a few moments before it appeared on the trestle bridge over the river, near the edge of Bee Tree Hill property. Chase walked onto the pier and pulled his phone out of his back pocket before sitting on a stone bench.

It was only five in the morning in Seattle, but his father would be awake. The man hardly slept. In his mind, sleep was a waste of time and he'd conditioned his body to run on three or four hours a night. Work was the fuel that kept Malcolm Asher alive.

Chase set his cup of coffee on the bench and stared at his phone. He hadn't slept much the night before, either, but it was because he'd spent the hours thinking about Joy and his girls—*his* girls. It still seemed like a dream. How could he be a dad? And how could he have been living carefree for the past four years while Joy had sacrificed everything to bring those girls into this world and then care for them?

He dropped his chin for a moment and closed his eyes, praying God would give him what it would take to be a good dad.

It would start with this phone call.

Taking a deep breath, Chase turned on his phone and tapped the green icon. He found his dad's number and touched it. Immediately, it began to ring and Chase lifted the phone to his ear, not willing himself to second-guess this decision.

"What's wrong?" his dad asked.

Chase waited for a heartbeat and then said, "Good morning, Dad."

"I haven't received any reports. What's taking you so long?"

"It's good to be back at Bee Tree Hill." Chase stood and put his free hand in his pocket as he watched the train. The morning was so clear, a perfect reflection of the trestle and the train mirrored in the river. "Did you ever spend time here?"

"What?" His dad's voice was tight and confused.

"Did Uncle Morgan ever tell you about the history of Bee Tree Hill? About your great-grandfather, John Asher? There has been an Asher living at Bee Tree Hill, and in Timber Falls, for over a hundred and twenty years. Our family made this town what it is today."

"What are you talking about, Chase? I don't have time for a trip down memory lane."

"I hate seeing this part of our family history sold to an investor."

"We're in the business of making money—not holding on to liabilities because of sentiment." His dad spoke as if he was walking on his treadmill—his words a bit breathy. "Uncle Morgan was fortunate that I didn't sell the place years ago and put him in a retirement ho—"

"What if I took over Bee Tree Hill?"

"It's out of the question. There is nothing left for the Asher family in Timber Falls. The lumber mill closed down almost seventy years ago. Uncle Morgan never even worked for the corporation. He was a bank president."

"I'd like—"

"I need you here in Seattle. One day, the Asher Corporation will need a new president and CEO and I want you to be ready."

It was the first time Dad had suggested that Chase would take over the corporation one day—and Chase wasn't sure how he felt about it. He had no wish to be married to the family business. His dad worked hard and never relaxed. He didn't take vacations, read books or spend time with friends and family. From morning until night, every day of the year, he was devoted to the business.

"With no income outside your work with the Asher Corporation, you could not afford to buy Bee Tree Hill

Mrs. Thompson nodded and smiled. She tilted her head toward the back stairs. "There's no harm in offering."

Chase turned toward the stairs and didn't give himself a chance to hesitate. He took the steps two at a time. When he got to the top, he turned right. The girls' bedroom door was open and Harper sat on the floor, her little legs straight out in front, a book on her lap. She still wore her footie pajamas, and her pigtails from the day before were crooked, but he'd never seen anything more adorable.

She looked up at him, her big brown eyes steady and watchful. Sunshine filtered through the billowy white curtains at the windows and bathed her in light.

Joy was nowhere to be seen or heard.

Chase stood at the door, unwilling to enter unless Harper was comfortable with him.

It wasn't the first time he'd seen her with a book. She often had one in her hand as she toddled about the house.

"What are you reading?" he asked, leaning against the doorframe.

"My Lucky Day." She lifted it off her lap. The front cover had a painting of a wolf staring down at a sheepish-looking pig. "You read?"

Was she asking him if he had read it—or if he'd read it to her?

He took a tentative step into her room. She didn't shy away—instead, she stood and reached up to him. He stopped—surprised that she wanted him to pick her up.

"You read?" she asked again.

"Do you want me to read to you?" he asked.

Harper nodded, her arms still raised.

His heart pounding, he reached down and picked up daughter. She was so soft and delicate, he was almost [a]id to hold her. What if he dropped her?

and I will never give it to you. Ashers work for what they want. Nothing in life is free."

Ashers work for what they want. He wanted to give Bee Tree Hill to his daughters. It was part of their legacy, and it was part of the legacy of Timber Falls. Just like Uncle Morgan had been allowed to live in the home, Chase wanted his girls to grow up on the estate—not because they had to work for it, but because he wanted it to be a gift.

But he'd never get it from his father. He'd have to buy it—and he had no money of his own—at least, not enough to purchase a multimillion-dollar estate.

"Why are you playing this game with me?" his dad asked. "You never told me you wanted Bee Tree Hill before."

Everything was a game to his father. In his mind, no one could ever have a pure motive. Even if Chase told him the truth, Dad would assume Joy was coercing him or Chase had a selfish reason for wanting the property. Even if he wanted to explain, his dad would never understand. Just like Joy, Chase was leery to tell his dad about the girls—at least for now. He needed to make sure Joy had secure housing before his dad ever learned the truth.

"It's not a game." Chase sighed as the train disappeared. "I just don't want the things you want. I like Timber Falls. I like Bee Tree Hill. I like our family legacy—"

"I don't have time for this. Do your job, Chase. This is the last time I'm telling you that. If you give me any more trouble, I'm pulling you out of there and I'll send in someone who could care less about Timber Falls and Bee Tree Hill."

The phone went dead. Chase stared at it for a minute, anger and frustration making his jaw tight. His father was at the head of the company and no one ever went against him. Even if Chase called all the board members and made his plea with them, they'd never side with Chase. They were too afraid of Malcolm.

But he couldn't give up. Even if he failed, he had to show Joy that he was on her side. He'd fight with her to the end, if he needed to, and he wouldn't give up on his desire to give Bee Tree Hill to his daughters.

Shoving his phone back into his pocket, he grabbed his cup of coffee and started toward the mansion. More than anything, he wanted to see the girls again. He didn't know when Joy would tell them he was their father, but that didn't change the fact that he knew.

The heavy kitchen door was open and the sounds of breakfast drifted out of the enclosed porch. Constant chatter, pots clanging on the stove, and chairs scraping across the floor mingled with the sounds of birds calling in the trees and ducks quacking in the nearby pond. Chase didn't usually come for breakfast, but he would now. If Joy would have him, he'd be there for every meal.

But as he reached for the screen door, his pulse started to race and his palms grew moist. What would he say? How would Joy treat him? What did a dad do?

"Is that you, Chase?" Mrs. Thompson called from the kitchen. "Will you set the garbage bags in the bins by the back door?"

Through the screen, he saw two full kitchen garbage bags sitting in the porch. He opened the door, picked them up and then walked them outside to the bins. The simple, everyday act made his pulse settle and his mind clear.

"Ryan, could you set a plate for Chase?" Mrs. Thompson asked as Chase opened the screen door and stepped into the porch.

"Morning, Chase!" Ryan called.

"Morning, Chase!" Jordan, Kodi and Kinsley echoed.

He smiled as he stepped over the threshol[d] bustling kitchen. Mrs. Thompson stood at the st[ove] t[ting] warm bacon onto a plate covered with a pape[r] Ryan stood on a step stool near a cabinet, reach[ing] a plate, Jordan had a pitcher of orange juice an[d] pouring it into all the cups and Kodi was setting kins at each place. Kinsley was in her booster, a M[in]nie Mouse bib around her neck, a big-handled fork [and] spoon in each fist.

Kinsley was the first to greet him with a gri[n] "Chase!" She wiggled in her booster chair, pure delight on her sweet face.

Chase couldn't take his eyes off her. It was one thing to know she was Joy's daughter—another entirely to see her as his.

"You want bacon?" she asked.

He wanted to pull her into his arms and hold her close—but he just nodded.

"I like bacon." She clapped her fists together when Mrs. Thompson turned from the stove and set the platter of bacon on the table. "You like bacon?" Kinsle[y] asked Chase.

"I love bacon."

She squealed and he laughed.

The child knew what she liked—and did not [like] when it came to food.

"Good morning," Mrs. Thompson said wit[h a] s[mile] She winked at Chase. The way she looked [at him] suspected that Joy had told her about their c[onversation].

"Joy is getting Harper dressed," Mrs. Th[ompson said] "She might like it if you go up and help."

"Help?" Would Joy like that? Or woul[d she think it] an intrusion?

his afra[id]

She pointed to a rocking chair in the corner where two floor-to-ceiling windows came together.

Chase walked to the rocker and took a seat. She positioned herself on his lap and opened the book to the first page.

The top of her head came up to his chin, and when she settled back against his chest, her wayward pigtail tickled his cheek.

He started to read the story, and she giggled at the silly pig that accidentally came to the wolf's house.

As Chase read, he laughed at the funny story and got into the characters, changing his voice and reacting along with the pig and the wolf. Harper's eyes shined as she looked up at him, her smile brighter than the morning, and Chase thought his chest would burst from the love he felt for her.

How was it possible to love someone so much in such a short amount of time?

When he finished the story, Harper clapped and said, "Again!"

"It's time for breakfast." Joy stood in the doorway, Harper's clothes in hand.

Chase and Harper looked up at the same moment. How long had she been standing there?

Joy had not expected Chase to come to the main house until later in the day. But here he sat, his broad shoulders and long legs making the rocking chair look like doll's furniture, with their daughter on his lap. Harper stared up at him with stars in her eyes and laughter on her lips.

The scene took Joy's breath away.

But *My Lucky Day* was Harper's favorite book, and if Joy didn't put a stop to it now, she'd have Chase read it to her half a dozen times—and with the look of wonder on his face, he'd probably agree.

"Again!" Harper said to Chase.

"Your mama wants you to eat breakfast." Chase didn't make a move to set her on her feet. "But I'll read to you later, if you'd like."

"Yes." With that promise, Harper climbed off Chase's lap.

"Can you thank Chase for reading to you?" Joy asked her.

The little girl turned. "Thank you."

Chase sat with his hands on the armrests and smiled at their daughter. "You're welcome."

Then Harper ran to Joy to get dressed.

"Do you need help?" Chase asked, coming to her side.

"I think we'll be okay." She unzipped Harper's pajamas and helped the little girl step out, then she put on her purple jean shorts and white tank top with the purple hearts. The entire time, Harper talked about the pig in the story.

"Mrs. Thompson has breakfast on the table," Joy said to Harper as she lifted her into her arms, "so we'll fix your hair later."

"How do you do it?" Chase asked Joy.

"Do what?"

"Selflessly get up every morning and take care of all their needs."

Many people asked Joy that question, and she had a canned answer. "What choice do I have?"

"You have a lot of choices. Not everyone would take in three little boys while juggling twins as a single mom." He put his hands in his pockets and lifted a shoulder. "Not everyone chooses to be a mom. I admire you, because you've not only chosen to be a mom, but you've chosen to be a good one."

His words should have been a compliment, but instead they hurt. Her mom was one of those people who had chosen not to be a mother. When her dad left, Joy had been seven and it had destroyed her mom. Within two years, her mom had also left. Joy had been nine when the county learned that she'd been living alone for over a month. There was no food in the house, the water and electricity had been turned off and the neighbors had started to complain about the unkempt yard. "I know what it feels like to be a lonely and unwanted child," she said, "and no matter how much I have to sacrifice, I will never, ever make these children feel how I felt." She set Harper down and said, "Go to the kitchen for your breakfast, sweetie."

Harper skipped out of the room, hopping from one foot to the next with little coordination, and went to the stairs where she held the railing and grinned at Chase before disappearing.

Joy turned to Chase. She'd already opened her heart to tell him the truth about the girls. Why not be honest about the boys, too? "When I heard that the boys were in need of a home, and I had one, I couldn't turn them away. I knew it would be a lot of work, and I knew it would be frustrating and painful at times—and that people might doubt my ability—but I also knew I had enough love for all of them." The last foster home Joy had lived in before graduating from high school was the one where she learned what unconditional love felt like. And when she'd moved into Morgan Asher's home to work for the summer, she'd encountered it again in Uncle Morgan and Mr. and Mrs. Thompson. She wanted to offer that same love to as many foster children as she could.

"I think what you're doing for the boys—and the girls—is wonderful," Chase said.

His eyes were so full of warmth and admiration, she swallowed uncomfortably. "We should probably get to the kitchen to help Mrs. Thompson."

"Wait." He reached out and touched her arm to stop her from turning. "I didn't sleep much last night."

His touch, coupled with his intimate words, made her shiver. She hadn't slept, either. She'd been too overwhelmed with the knowledge that she'd told him the truth—and now wondered when she should tell the girls.

"I called my father today," he said.

Dread and fear took hold of her throat and squeezed until she felt like she would choke. "Why?"

"I asked him for Bee Tree Hill."

"Did you tell him about the girls?"

"No." He frowned and shook his head. "I have no reason to tell him—I'm still trying to process the information myself. The last thing I need is his interference."

She started to breathe easier, allowing his other statement to finally hit her. "You asked him to give you the estate?"

"He said he wouldn't give it to me—but, Joy, now that I know about Harper and Kinsley, I'm even more certain that you should raise the girls here, if that's what you want. It's their family home."

She had never wanted anything more. "What are you saying?"

"That I'm reaffirming my commitment to help you stay at Bee Tree Hill. I still have to keep my father happy, or he'll send someone else to do the job, but I want you to know that I will not let this place go without a fight. You have my word."

It took Joy a moment, but she finally nodded, her heart

nudging her to put her trust in him again. She knew Chase didn't have the power to keep Bee Tree Hill—didn't know that he'd even be successful at his goal—but what he was asking her to do was trust that he'd exhaust every possibility.

"I appreciate your offer, Chase, but I told you yesterday that you don't need to feel obligat—"

"They're my daughters, Joy." The lines of his face were serious. "I want to be their dad."

She inhaled. For the past four years, she'd wanted the same thing.

"It's more than obligation," he said, shaking his head in wonder. "I already love those girls more than life itself. I want to be the dad I never had—I want to be a part of their life. Not just this summer—but forever."

Tears stung the backs of her eyes. Was Chase capable of being that kind of dad? She used to think so—a long time ago before he'd proven otherwise.

His hands were still in the pockets of his khaki pants, and he suddenly looked like a younger, less confident version of himself. "That means you might have to get used to me being around."

Joy swallowed the flutter that raced up her throat at his words, feeling like a younger, more uncomfortable version of herself, as well. Could she get used to him being around? How could she keep her old feelings buried, if he continued to resurrect them? Could she keep her heart from being broken again?

But what if he was trustworthy? What if he was a great dad? Didn't she need to risk that for her daughters' sake?

"I think I could get used to it again." She crossed her arms, not knowing what to do with them as she ran her toe along a design in the carpet. "For Harper's and Kinsley's sakes."

There was an awkward pause and Joy finally looked up at him.

He was so good-looking, it hurt.

"I should probably help Mrs. Thompson," she said.

"The appraiser should be here any minute," he said at the same time.

"Okay." She had the urge to hug him—or at least shake hands—or something. They had come to some sort of agreement about their daughters—shouldn't that be marked by affection?

No.

She forced herself to turn away from Chase. The last thing she needed from him was physical touch.

Chapter Eight

The red Mazda drove slowly around the circle drive and came to a stop in front of the mansion where Chase waited. Inside the car, the driver put the vehicle in Park, turned off the engine and then opened the door.

Chase walked around the front of the car and extended his hand. "You must be Mr. Taylor."

Mr. Taylor nodded and his glasses slid down the bridge of his nose. He quickly pushed them up before shaking Chase's hand.

"I am Mr. Taylor." The man smiled and his small mustache lifted at the corners. "And you're Mr. Asher?"

"Chase." He indicated the house. "Welcome to Bee Tree Hill."

Mr. Taylor's small eyes were made bigger behind his thick glasses as he studied the place. His brown hair was thin on top and he wore the sides longer, combing it over to compensate. He wore a pair of brown pants, which were too short, and a brown-striped shirt which was so thin and worn, Chase could easily make out the white shirt underneath.

"I'm sure the house is full of treasures, yet to be discovered," Mr. Taylor said, rubbing his hands together. "I'm eager to get to work."

"Did you find the hotel?" Chase asked.

"Yes, yes. Thank you." Mr. Taylor opened the passenger door and pulled out a worn briefcase. "If you'll point me in the right direction, I'd like to start as soon as possible. You're paying me by the hour, you know."

"Yes, I know." Chase pointed to the stairs that led up to the enclosed porch. "I set up a card table in the porch, just like you asked. There is a family living here and it was the most convenient space I could find, so you will have a quiet place to work."

"Good, good." Mr. Taylor followed Chase up the stairs.

The man had come highly recommended by the local historical society, who had worked with him on several projects over the years.

Chase showed him his work space and where he could plug in his laptop. "How long do you think the job will take?"

"I can't say for sure until I've had a chance to explore the house a bit. But," he looked around at the covered porch and then out the window at the side of the house, "by my estimations, taking in the size of the exterior and the information you've given me about how old the house and artifacts are," Chase could almost see the numbers being calculated in the man's head, "I think it could take me three or four weeks to properly document and value the items—unless you need me to do it faster."

"No." Chase shook his head. The longer it took the better. "Please, take your time and do not feel rushed for any reason. We want a thorough and complete list and valuation."

Mr. Taylor set his bag on the table. "And the family you told me about, will they feel like I'm intruding?"

"I've spoken to them and they know what to expect. They will do everything they can to accommodate you— but they have asked that you let them know what room you'll be working in each day, so they can keep the children out of your way."

"That won't be a problem."

Chase's phone rang. He pulled it from his back pocket and didn't recognize the number. "Do you mind if I answer this, and then I can take you on a tour?"

"Of course," Mr. Taylor said, waving Chase off. "I have a few more things to get from my car." He left the porch and closed the door.

Chase tapped the green phone icon and answered the call. "Hello," he said.

"Is this Chase Asher?" the man on the other end asked.

"It is."

"My name is Conrad Tidwell. Your father gave me your number and said I should call you to schedule a visit to see the property."

Frowning, Chase walked to the far side of the porch and looked out at the pond. "I'm sorry—I'm not sure—"

"I am interested in purchasing the estate. I'm in Singapore right now, and it looks like my trip will not last as long as I had planned. I should arrive in San Francisco in mid-July and can be in Minnesota a few days later."

Mid-July wasn't enough time. They had already started to advertise the Bee Tree Hill Festival for July twenty-seventh.

"I have just started the appraisal work," Chase said, trying to think of a way to stall Mr. Tidwell's arrival. "I don't think we'll be ready to show the place until the beginning of August at the earliest."

"I'm not overly concerned about the appraisal," said Mr. Tidwell. "My biggest concerns are its location, the size of the community and the access to the river. Could you text pictures of the property to this number?"

"There is a family currently living here," Chase told Mr. Tidwell. "They have until the end of July to vacate the premises. I will take as many photos as I can, but I cannot schedule a showing with you until after the first of August."

There was a pause on the other end. "I was under the impression that Malcolm wanted to sell the property as soon as possible."

"He does." If his dad knew he was threatening this sale, he'd replace Chase within twenty-four hours, so he needed to play it safe. "But we were not aware of the family living here until I arrived. It was my late uncle's wish that the family was taken care of, so we are trying to accommodate that request. I am happy to send you pictures and any other information you may need, but I cannot show the property to you until August."

Again, another pause. "Fine. I will plan for August then. I'll be in touch in the coming weeks to tell you my arrival time. And I look forward to seeing those pictures."

"Thank you for calling." Chase ended the call just as Mr. Taylor reentered the porch. Chase stepped over to the door and held it open for the older man. "Do you need help?"

"No, no." Mr. Taylor carried a large brown box into the house. "I'm fine."

Chase's mind was no longer on the appraiser or the tour he needed to give. Instead, he was thinking about Mr. Tidwell and the impending visit. If Tidwell didn't purchase the property, then someone else would. It was only a matter of time, which meant that Chase had to come up with money fast.

He had a little amount in savings—nothing close to

what he'd need to purchase the house—but what about a bank? Maybe a hometown bank, knowing Chase's connection to the property, would be willing to take a risk on him—but how would he possibly make the monthly payment on a multimillion-dollar loan? There was a chance that someday, if he was the CEO of the Asher Corporation, he could afford it—but on his current salary, there was no way.

"I think I'm ready for that tour, Mr. Asher." Mr. Taylor grinned.

"Please, call me Chase."

"Then please call me Ernie."

Chase nodded and showed Ernie into the front foyer.

When he had a chance, Chase would make a trip to the bank. Even if it seemed unlikely, he had to try. If nothing else, maybe the banker would have a better idea.

A week after Joy had told Chase about the girls, she sat in the parking lot of the Government Center, rain pattering against the windshield of Mrs. Thompson's old Prius. It was Wednesday and Mrs. Thompson had volunteered to bring the children to church that evening, so Joy had left her the minivan and she had taken the smaller car in case her meetings ran late—which they had.

She had just left a meeting with the boys' caseworker and could not bring herself to turn on the car. The news she would need to deliver to Ryan, Jordan and Kodi would break their hearts. There would be no more visits for the boys and their birth mom. She had left the state without contacting her caseworker and had dropped out of her treatment program. She had broken her paternity agreement, thereby nullifying her parental rights. All that was needed was a judge to sign the official papers.

It was the final act of abandonment in their short lives

and Joy prayed it would be the last. She had already spoken to the social worker about her wish to adopt the boys, and the social worker said she would start the process. There were still many things that needed to happen, and many months that would pass before their case was brought before a judge. Thankfully, she already had her foster license, which was the longest step in the adoption process.

But if she didn't have a house for them, there was no way the judge would allow her to adopt those boys.

Maybe it was time to start looking at her other options. The last thing she wanted was to leave Bee Tree Hill, but if she had no other choice, then maybe she should look at other properties.

Turning on the engine, Joy flipped the wipers on and backed the car out of the parking space. She was so weary, she didn't want to think about her housing problem tonight—or any other problem, for that matter— but she would need to work on another grant application when she returned to the house.

The rain began to fall harder and it became more difficult to see the road.

Pulling into Bee Tree Hill, Joy noticed Mr. Taylor's Mazda was not parked in his regular spot near the house. The little man had become a welcome fixture in their daily lives. They didn't interact very often, but he did join them for their afternoon meals and he was a pleasant conversationalist. Joy had always been fascinated by history, and this man was a walking historical resource. Not only did he share the history about Bee Tree Hill that he came across, he was also an expert on Minnesota history, as well.

Joy pulled into her spot along the north side of the

mansion and put the car in Park. She turned off the engine and heard her phone ding.

Lifting her purse onto her lap, she took out her phone. The rain continued to pour, sending a torrent of water down the eaves of the house and into the lawn. She could hardly see the Mississippi in the distance because of the downpour.

When she pressed the home button on her phone, the message notification showed her the email was from the organization she'd sent her first grant application to. It had only been a week and a half, so she doubted she'd have an answer, but maybe they had another question to ask.

She tapped the email and scanned it—but then she paused and went back to read the whole thing.

The board had met the day after they received her application and they were pleased to tell her they would award her twenty-five thousand dollars to put toward her housing needs.

Joy stared at the screen, her mouth slipping open in surprise.

Twenty-five thousand dollars?

It wasn't nearly enough money to purchase Bee Tree Hill, but it was still a substantial amount.

Hope sprang afresh in her heart and she grinned. This was just the beginning—her first grant application— hopefully it was an indication of things yet to come.

She didn't even care that it was raining and she'd get wet. She tossed her phone into her purse, opened the door and rushed out of the car. Giggling, she ran through several puddles and up the back stairs into the enclosed porch just off the kitchen. She hadn't felt this light or optimistic for months. Even with the news of the boys' mother, which wasn't all that surprising, all she could do was thank God for the many blessings in her life.

The smell of chili wafted on the air as Joy closed the back door. She hung her purse on the hook and pulled off her light summer coat. Had Mrs. Thompson made her supper before leaving for church? She didn't need to do that. Joy would have been happy with a bowl of cereal.

Pushing open the inner door, Joy stopped short when she found Chase standing at the stove, stirring something in a pot.

A flash of lightning lit up the dark sky and was quickly followed by thunder.

Chase looked up from the stove to glance out the window and found Joy standing there.

"Hello," he said.

"Hello."

A timer went off and Chase tore his gaze from Joy's to open the oven. A pan of cornbread sat in the middle of the rack, its edges golden brown.

"You're just in time for supper." He pulled a potholder from a drawer and took out the cornbread. "Are you hungry?"

She was famished. She hadn't eaten since breakfast, which had been a hurried cup of coffee and a granola bar as she left the house early that morning. Her stomach took that moment to growl.

Heat warmed her face. "My stomach cannot tell a lie." She laughed, feeling more carefree than she could ever remember. "Did Mrs. Thompson make that before she left?"

Chase shook his head and set the cornbread on the table. "It's my own recipe. I hope you don't mind that I used the kitchen."

How could she mind? "I didn't know you cooked."

"I've been living on my own for a while." He shrugged. "You either cook or eat out, and since I like being home as much as possible, I learned to cook."

He went to the cupboard and pulled out two bowls, then he took them to the stove and started to dish up.

Joy wasn't certain it was smart to have a quiet meal alone with Chase, but she didn't know how to back out now—and, if she was being honest with herself, she didn't want to back out. Despite everything between them, she still enjoyed Chase's company—and had even found herself looking forward to seeing him.

She went to the refrigerator and took out some shredded cheddar cheese and sour cream. "Do you like crackers or tortilla chips in your chili?" she asked him.

"Chips."

She opened the pantry and took out a bag and then met him back at the table, where he'd set the steaming bowls of chili, along with silverware.

They stood facing each other for a second.

Another bolt of lightning was followed by more thunder. It rattled the windows and reverberated in her chest.

She recalled another summer afternoon, about four years ago, when she and Chase had been at Bee Tree Hill alone during a thunderstorm. The thrill of being with someone who made her feel beautiful and wanted had rendered her numb to all reason. Chase could have asked her to climb Mount Everest that day, and she would have tried. She'd felt so invincible, so full of life, she'd compromised her better judgment and fallen in love with a man she had believed was different than all the others.

But *was* he like all the others? Or had he simply made one bad decision? She'd made bad decisions before—did she want her poor choices to determine how people felt about her?

His eyes were full as he looked at her and she wondered if he was remembering that long-ago evening, as well. They had talked and laughed and shared their greatest dreams with one another. It seemed like a lifetime ago.

Chase pulled out his chair and she did the same. They sat and faced each other across the table.

"Should I pray?" he asked quietly.

Joy nodded.

There was a brief hesitation and then he reached across the table with his right hand.

She also hesitated, but then she extended her left and he grasped her hand in his. Their eyes met momentarily and then she closed hers and bowed her head.

His skin was warm and the sensation of his thumb as he brushed it across the top of her hand sent pleasure up her arm and into her chest. Her cheeks burned as she tried to focus on his prayer.

"Lord," he began slowly, as if he needed a moment to catch his breath, "we thank You for this food, for this home and for each and every blessing You've given us." He paused. "And, Lord, we pray You show us the way to make Bee Tree Hill a permanent home and safe haven for Joy and the kids. Amen."

"Amen," she whispered in agreement.

She opened her eyes and met Chase's gaze just before he released her hand.

"I have good news," she said, a little more cheerful than she expected to sound after his solemn prayer.

He took a dollop of sour cream and mixed it into his chili. "What's that?"

"I received one of the grants I applied for. I'll be awarded twenty-five thousand dollars to help with housing."

"Joy, that's amazing!" His face lit up and his blue eyes sparkled.

"It's not much—"

"It's more than you had."

"But I can use it for any form of housing I choose—I just have to report to the board where I use it."

"What do you mean, any form of housing?"

"If I have to find another house in town—I don't have to use it for Bee Tree Hill—I just have to use it to house my foster children."

He stopped crumbling chips into his bowl. "Are you thinking about looking for a different house?"

She shrugged. "I don't know what else to do. If we don't stay at Bee Tree Hill—"

"I went to the bank today," he interrupted. "I applied for a mortgage loan."

Her heart started to pound a little harder. "What did you learn?"

"I qualify for a loan." He wiped his hands on a napkin, his face serious. "But it will only be about a quarter of what we'll need."

She didn't know how she felt about Chase taking out such a substantial loan for her and the girls. "How would you afford to live somewhere else if you're making payments on a loan for Bee Tree Hill?"

"Let me worry about that."

"But, you don't need to—"

"I do."

His answer held no room for argument—but it didn't matter. If she couldn't come up with the other three-quarters, she'd still not have enough.

"I still need to look for alternative housing. Six weeks isn't a long time to find somewhere to move." Suddenly, the food didn't look so appetizing. "Now that I think about it, I should probably start packing."

"No." Chase shook his head. "I don't care what my

father says. You don't need to leave on August first. If we don't have all the funding we need by the end of July, you can start packing then. Even if my dad sells the place, it'll take several weeks for the sale to be completed."

"I can't keep relying on what-if." She used the knife Chase had brought to the table and cut the cornbread into squares. "I had other news today that will affect my future."

Chase set down his spoon and frowned. "What?"

"The boys' mom left the state, which means she's given up her rights." She paused as she let the news sink in. "I've started the adoption process."

He didn't respond right away, and she knew he was struggling with what to say. It was a bittersweet moment. It was heartbreaking to know a mother was being permanently separated from her children—yet there was hope because another forever family was being born.

"I'm sorry about their mom," he finally said. "But I'm excited for you and for them."

"That's why I cannot wait—"

The doorbell rang, interrupting Joy's words.

Frowning, she stood. Chase also stood and followed her out of the kitchen and into the front foyer.

Joy opened the foyer door and found Pastor Jacob Dawson standing on the front step in the rain.

"Oh, goodness!" Joy rushed to the other door and opened it. "Come in, Pastor!"

Pastor Jacob grinned at Joy, his smile wide and bright with matching dimples. He stepped into the porch, his black shoes squeaking from the water. He was a tall man with the kindest eyes Joy had ever seen. He'd been a constant support to her and Mrs. Thompson over the past two years, and his seven-year-old daughter Maggie was one of Ryan's best friends. As a widower, he'd come to

Timber Falls to start over and he'd been welcomed with open arms by the community.

"It's Wednesday. I thought you'd be at church." Joy closed the door behind him.

"I'm on my way there now," he said in his calm and unhurried way. "I performed a small funeral at the nursing home this afternoon."

Pastor Jacob glanced toward Chase with a curious smile. For whatever reason, she felt embarrassed to be alone with Chase—and to be caught by the pastor, even though they had done nothing wrong.

"Pastor Jacob, this is—" She was at a loss to explain who Chase was. An old friend? The father of her children?

"Chase Asher," Chase said, stepping forward to shake the pastor's hand. "Morgan Asher was my great-uncle."

Pastor Jacob shook Chase's hand. "It's nice to meet you, Chase. Your uncle was one of our oldest members when he passed away, and the last of the Asher family to attend Timber Falls Community Church. It was your family that started the congregation almost a hundred and thirty years ago."

"Really?" Chase shook his head in amazement. "The more I learn about my ancestors, the more I like them."

"I actually stopped by with some good news, Joy." Pastor Jacob wore a long black coat and a black suit. He was probably ten years older than Joy, though he had a few more careworn wrinkles on his forehead and around his mouth than other men his age. He carried a heavy weight as a single father and a pastor, but he did it with such grace and patience, Joy wondered how he kept his easygoing manner.

"Good news?" she asked.

He smiled a bit uncomfortably at Chase, though he

didn't suggest they speak alone. "We heard about your housing situation," he said to her, "and I spoke to the elder board. We have agreed to take a special offering for you this Sunday at church and also give you the current balance available in the benevolent fund."

She stared at her pastor, uncertain what to say. "There are so many people in need in this community—I'd hate to take the benevolent money."

He waved away her fears. "The money is for those in need—and right now, that would be you and the children. You are a rock in church, so is Mrs. Thompson, and you both give so selflessly—plus, Morgan Asher was a faithful member who gave his tithes to the church his entire adult life. There was zero hesitation on the part of the board." He pulled a folded check from his pocket. "I wish it was more—but hopefully the congregation is generous on Sunday."

Joy glanced at Chase and then back at the pastor. "I don't know what to say."

"Say you'll take it for the children," Pastor Jacob told her.

Stepping forward, she took the check—and then hugged her pastor. "Thank you."

He returned the hug. "Some days, being a pastor is one of the hardest jobs I've ever had." He pulled back and smiled. "And then other days, like today, I get to do something that makes up for all those tough times."

Joy didn't even bother to look at the check, because it didn't matter what the number said. It was a gift from people who loved her and her family unconditionally. To her, the gift was priceless. Tears stung the backs of her eyes. "Are you hungry? Would you like to join us for chili?"

"No, thank you. I haven't seen Mags today and I'd like to eat with her at church."

Joy nodded in understanding and then opened the door for Pastor Jacob to leave. "Thanks again."

He grinned and nodded at Chase. "We'll see you later."

"Goodbye," Chase said. "It was nice to meet you."

"You, too." Pastor Jacob left the porch and darted through the rain to his waiting car.

Joy closed the door and faced Chase, the seed of hope growing stronger with each gift.

"He seems like a good guy," Chase said.

"One of the best." And not only because he was her pastor, but because he was one of those men who truly loved his congregation as Christ loved the church. He'd taught her so much in the past two years, she was beyond grateful that he'd answered the call to come to Timber Falls.

"The more time I spend in Timber Falls," Chase said as he leaned against the doorframe, his arms crossed, "the more I like it." He met her gaze with an emotion she couldn't identify. "I'm happy you're raising the girls here. I wouldn't want it any other way."

Neither would she—she just hoped they could stay.

Chapter Nine

❧

"If Joy adopts me and is my forever mom," Ryan said to Chase the next day as they stood at the bottom of Bee Tree Hill and Chase used his phone to take pictures for Mr. Tidwell, "who will be my forever dad?"

The sun was already low in the sky and if Chase wanted to get enough pictures to satisfy Mr. Tidwell, he'd have to work fast. He'd already put off the task for too long and didn't want Tidwell contacting his father.

But Ryan's question deserved attention.

"I suppose that depends on who Joy marries one day." The thought of Joy marrying another man didn't sit well with Chase—especially when he thought about that man raising his daughters.

It was an altogether new thought and feeling—one he didn't like at all.

They stood near the gazebo, facing the back of the mansion. The river ran behind them with the setting sun sparkling off the water.

Ryan picked up a stick and absently broke it in half. "What if the man she marries doesn't want us?"

Chase put down his phone and squatted to look at Ryan, eye to eye. Right now it wasn't about Chase and

"One Minute" Survey

You get up to **FOUR books** <u>and</u> Mystery Gifts...

> **ABSOLUTELY FREE!**

Romance

YOU pick your books – WE pay for everything!

Suspense

See inside for details.

YOU pick your books –
WE pay for everything.
You get up to FOUR new books and TWO Mystery Gifts..
absolutely FREE!
Total retail value: Over $20!

Dear Reader,

Your opinions are important to us. So if you'll participate in our fast and free "One Minute" Survey, **YOU** can pick up to four wonderful books that **WE** pay for!

As a leading publisher of women's fiction, we'd love to hear from you. That's why we promise to reward you for completing our survey.

IMPORTANT: Please complete the survey and return it. We'll send your Free Books and Free Mystery Gifts right away. **And we pay for shipping and handling too!** *We pay for EVERYTHING!*

Try **Love Inspired® Romance Larger-Print** books and fall in love with inspirational romances that take you on an uplifting journey of faith, forgiveness and hope.

Try **Love Inspired® Suspense Larger-Print** books where courage and optimism unite in stories of faith and love in the face of danger.

Or TRY BOTH!

Thank you again for participating in our "One Minute" Survey. It really takes just a minute (or less) to complete the survey… and your free books and gifts will be well worth it!

Sincerely,

Pam Powers

Pam Powers
for Reader Service

www.ReaderService.com

"One Minute" Survey

GET YOUR FREE BOOKS AND FREE GIFTS!

✓ Complete this Survey ✓ Return this survey

▶ DETACH AND MAIL CARD TODAY!

1 Do you try to find time to read every day?
☐ YES ☐ NO

2 Do you prefer books which reflect Christian values?
☐ YES ☐ NO

3 Do you enjoy having books delivered to your home?
☐ YES ☐ NO

4 Do you find a Larger Print size easier on your eyes?
☐ YES ☐ NO

YES! I have completed the above "One Minute" Survey. Please send me my Free Books and Free Mystery Gifts (worth over $20 retail). I understand that I am under no obligation to buy anything, as explained on the back of this card.

☐ I prefer Love Inspired Romance Larger Print 122/322 IDL GNP4
☐ I prefer Love Inspired Suspense Larger Print 107/307 IDL GNP4
☐ I prefer BOTH 122/322 & 107/307 IDL GNQG

FIRST NAME

LAST NAME

ADDRESS

APT.#

CITY

STATE/PROV.

ZIP/POSTAL CODE

Offer limited to one per household and not applicable to series that subscriber is currently receiving.
Your Privacy—The Reader Service is committed to protecting your privacy. Our Privacy Policy is available online at www.ReaderService.com or upon request from the Reader Service. We make a portion of our mailing list available to reputable third parties that offer products we believe may interest you. If you prefer that we not exchange your name with third parties, or if you wish to clarify or modify your communication preferences, please visit us at www.ReaderService.com/consumerschoice or write to us at Reader Service Preference Service, P.O. Box 9062, Buffalo, NY 14240-9062. Include your complete name and address.   LI/SLI-220-OMLR20

© 2019 HARLEQUIN ENTERPRISES ULC
™ and ® are trademarks owned by Harlequin Enterprises ULC. Printed in the U.S.A.

READER SERVICE—Here's how it works:

Accepting your 2 free books and 2 free gifts (gifts valued at approximately $10.00 retail) places you under no obligation to buy anything. You may keep the books and gifts and return the shipping statement marked "cancel." If you do not cancel, approximately one month later we'll send you 6 more books from each series you have chosen, and bill you at our low, subscribers-only discount price. Love Inspired® Romance Larger-Print books and Love Inspired® Suspense Larger-Print books consist of 6 books each month and cost just $5.99 each in the U.S. or $6.24 each in Canada. That is a savings of at least 17% off the cover price. It's quite a bargain! Shipping and handling is just 50¢ per book in the U.S. and $1.25 per book in Canada*. You may return any shipment at our expense and cancel at any time — or you may continue to receive monthly shipments at our low, subscribers-only discount price plus shipping and handling. *Terms and prices subject to change without notice. Prices do not include sales taxes which will be charged (if applicable) based on your state or country of residence. Canadian residents will be charged applicable taxes. Offer not valid in Quebec. Books received may not be as shown. All orders subject to approval. Credit or debit balances in a customer's account(s) may be offset by any other outstanding balance owed by or to the customer. Please allow 3 to 4 weeks for delivery. Offer available while quantities last.

▲ If offer card is missing write to: Reader Service, P.O. Box 1341, Buffalo, NY 14240-8531 or visit www.ReaderService.com ▲

BUSINESS REPLY MAIL
FIRST-CLASS MAIL   PERMIT NO. 717   BUFFALO, NY

POSTAGE WILL BE PAID BY ADDRESSEE

READER SERVICE
PO BOX 1341
BUFFALO NY 14240-8571

NO POSTAGE
NECESSARY
IF MAILED
IN THE
UNITED STATES

his feelings—he needed to reassure Ryan. "Joy would never marry someone who doesn't love you as much as he loves her."

"What if I don't like *him*?" Ryan asked, squinting one eye.

"Buddy, you don't have to worry about this." Chase put his phone in his back pocket, giving his entire attention to the little boy who carried far too many concerns for a child his age. "God has a special plan for your life. The first part of that plan was bringing you to live with Joy. Only He knows the future. You don't have to worry about what will happen. Joy, Mrs. Thompson and I will not let anyone hurt you—and Joy would never, ever marry someone who wasn't kind and good, just like her."

Ryan looked at the river for a second, his eyes flickering with his thoughts. "What if I don't get a forever dad?"

Chase wanted to pull Ryan into his arms and promise him that his life would be perfect, that he would get everything he hoped for—but life was messy, unpredictable and wasn't always fair. The best he could do was speak the truth in love. "Unfortunately, not everyone does."

Three ducks flew overhead and settled into the water nearby with a splash of their wings.

"But I want one," Ryan said quietly. "A lot of the kids at my school have dads."

"I wish you had a dad, too—but right now, I'm just thankful you have a mom who loves you with all her heart. And, if she'll let me, I'd like to do things with you—like build your fort—that a dad gets to do with his son."

Ryan nodded, acting much older than his eight years. "Thanks, Chase. But I don't think it's the same thing."

"I know, buddy." He put his hand on Ryan's shoulder, not having the heart to keep taking pictures.

Ryan looked up at him, hope shining from his face. "Could you marry Joy and be my forever dad?"

Chase was quiet for a second, remembering the last time he'd asked Joy to marry him. She had said yes, but then he'd left her without warning the very next day. He doubted she'd ever say yes to him again. "I don't think Joy would marry me."

"Yes, she would." Ryan nodded vigorously. "She likes you."

Chase grinned. "It takes a little more than that." He didn't want to encourage the conversation any further. "How about we head back to the house and see if supper is ready?"

"Okay."

They walked across the sprawling back lawn and up the stone steps to the back of the house, talking about their plans for the tree fort. They finally had the walls up and would work on the roof next. The boys were being patient, though Chase knew they itched to get it done— and he wanted it to be finished so they had time to enjoy it before the end of July.

A silver Porsche sat parked next to the back door near Joy's minivan.

Tom Winston was visiting again.

Chase tried to school his features as they entered the kitchen and found Mrs. Thompson making a cold pasta salad for supper.

"Where is everyone?" Chase asked.

"Mr. Taylor just left for the evening, Joy and the girls are in the dining room with Tom—and I think the younger boys are playing with Legos in their bedroom."

"Do you need help with supper?" Chase asked— though he'd rather go into the dining room to see why Tom had stopped by.

"I'm just finishing up this salad and then we'll be ready to eat." She looked at Ryan. "But I think it's your turn to set the table, young man."

Ryan moaned and went to the sink to wash his hands.

Chase didn't want to look too eager to check on Joy and Tom—but Mrs. Thompson was perceptive, and she nodded her head toward the dining room door. "Why don't you tell them supper will be on the table in five minutes?"

Chase grabbed a piece of pepperoni from her fixings and gave her a wink. "If you insist."

Pushing open the swinging door, he walked through the butler's pantry and through another swinging door into the dining room.

Joy and Tom sat side by side, a laptop open before them, while Harper and Kinsley sat across from them with their crayons and coloring books.

"Chase!" Kinsley said, standing up on her chair. She grabbed her coloring book and held it for him to see. "I colored a chicken."

"Sit on your bottom, Kinney," Joy told the little girl.

Kinsley plopped back down on the chair, but she didn't take her eyes off Chase. "You like my chicken?"

Chase circled the table and looked at her coloring. "I do like your chicken—especially its purple wings."

"Mama likes chickens," Harper supplied, holding up her own coloring book. It was a book of barnyard animals. "I color a chicken, too."

"You both did a great job," he told the girls and then looked up at Joy. "I didn't know you liked chickens."

She shrugged. "I visited a farm once when I was a little girl with my mom—ever since then I've wanted chickens."

"There's an old chicken coop near the barn at the bottom of the hill," Chase said. "You could have chickens if you wanted."

Joy shook her head and tried to laugh it off. "It's just a silly childhood dream."

It wasn't silly. He imagined it was one of the happiest memories Joy had with her mom and she'd somehow connected that with her love of chickens.

"Hello, Chase," Tom said.

Chase nodded a greeting. "You two look busy."

They sat so close, their arms brushed one another as they looked at the laptop.

Joy didn't meet Chase's gaze. "Tom agreed to help me find alternative housing."

"I told you not to worry about that right now," Chase said.

"It's always a good idea to have options." Tom crossed his arms. He wore a suit and his hair was combed to perfection. "If she wants to adopt those boys, she needs a place to live—and since you can't guarantee that she can stay here, then I'll help her find somewhere else to live."

"I'd guarantee it, if I could." Chase crossed his own arms. "But you don't need to help—Joy has me to do that now."

Joy's head came up and she frowned. "I asked Tom to help me."

He'd misspoken—taken a liberty with Joy that she had not offered. He had no right to make any claims on her, whether he was the father of her daughters or not. But he couldn't stand back and watch Tom weasel his way in, either. "Joy, if you needed help, you could have asked me."

"You told me I didn't need to look for another place, so I knew you wouldn't help." Her voice was tight. "That's why I asked Tom. He works with real estate all the time and has connections I don't."

Tom didn't speak, but he didn't need to. It was clear by the smug look on his face that he felt he had won this round—if that's what this was—a contest for Joy's affection.

But did Chase want Joy's affection?

If the jealousy he felt seeing Tom sidled up to her was any indication, he definitely didn't want someone else getting her affection. But did that mean he wanted it for himself?

The memory of holding her hand while they prayed the night before, and the pleasure he'd felt just being alone in her company while they ate, told him he did want her affection, more than he realized.

It was dangerous to question his feelings for Joy—not only because he'd recently come off a long engagement, but because he knew how Joy felt about him. Instead, he said, "Mrs. Thompson sent me in to tell you supper will be ready in a few minutes."

"Are we eating chicken?" Kinsley asked, wrinkling her nose.

Chase smiled for Kinsley and shrugged. "It's a surprise."

He took her out of the chair and set her on the ground, then he took Harper. "I'll help you wash up for supper."

Without looking back at Joy and Tom, he walked the girls out of the dining room and into the kitchen.

He couldn't stop Joy from spending time with Tom, but he could make Tom know he wasn't needed.

Two days later, on Saturday morning, Joy stood on the back porch with her mug of coffee and watched Chase build the tree fort with the boys. Earlier that morning, she'd woken up to the sound of hushed whispers as they snuck out of the house to work.

Now, as she watched, she smiled. Chase had frustrated her when Tom had been there to help the other night, but she knew he meant well. What was more frustrating, though, was the overwhelming lack of housing available in Timber Falls. Anything that was big enough for a family of seven was so run-down, there was no way she could fix it up and make it livable.

She and Tom had searched for hours, but Tom had left with no more answers than when he'd come.

As Joy watched the boys work on the tree fort, Ryan broke away from the group and ran up the long flight of stone stairs to the back of the house. He waved at Joy and came to the porch door. She had it open for him even before he clomped up the steps.

"Chase said I'm supposed to get you and the girls to come outside and help with a special project today."

If he wanted her to help with the fort, he would be disappointed. She had plans to work on more grants and she needed to do some cleaning, too. "What does he need help with?"

"He said it's a surprise." Ryan sighed impatiently.

Joy took another sip of her coffee. "Did you eat breakfast?"

"We took some bananas and granola bars with us to the fort." Ryan jumped from one foot to the other. "Come on, Mom!"

"Fine." She would see what the surprise was and then come back and work. "I'll get the girls and be there in a few minutes."

Ryan cheered and took off again.

The girls were just finishing their cereal in the kitchen, so Joy washed them up, put their bowls in the sink and then told Mrs. Thompson where they were going.

"Have fun," Mrs. Thompson called after her.

Joy walked down the hill with the girls at her side. The sun was bright, the air was warm and the earth smelled new and fresh. She held the girls' hands and hummed "How Great Is Our God" as they walked.

"They're coming!" Ryan called out to Chase when he caught sight of Joy and the girls.

There was a mad dash up the ladder as the boys disappeared inside their fort.

Chase stood at the bottom, his tool belt around his waist, a grin on his handsome face.

Just seeing him took her breath away. How long would it take for her to get used to him?

She focused her attention on the tree fort, instead. The three boys stood at a window and waved like mad at her.

With a squeal, the girls broke away from Joy and ran the rest of the way to Chase. He picked up Harper and tossed her in the air, and then he picked up Kinsley and did the same.

Joy's chest felt like it might burst at the sight of her five children and Chase, all of them happy and excited.

"Is the fort finished?" she asked when she was close enough.

"We just put in the last nail." Chase's face glowed with accomplishment. "We even put in a skylight."

Joy shielded her eyes with her hands to look up at the tree fort. "It's amazing."

"I go up?" Kinsley asked Chase, pulling on his hand.

"When the boys come down, I'll take you up," Chase told her. "But it's too small for all of us to go up at the same time."

"Is this your surprise?" Joy asked.

"Not quite." Chase's smile grew even wider, if that was possible. "I have a project for the family to do today."

The way he said *family* made Joy's heart speed up.

Somehow, in the past couple of weeks, whether she liked it or not, Chase had become a part of her family.

And she did like it—too much, in fact.

"Come down, boys," Chase called up to them. "Your sisters want to see inside."

The boys grumbled, but they came down, telling Joy all about the fort.

While they shared their excitement, Chase climbed up into the structure and looked down at Joy. "Can you help the girls up? I'll take them from here."

She nodded and helped Kinsley up the ladder first, handing her off to Chase. Then she helped Harper. It wasn't terribly far from the ground to the tree fort, but it was far enough that Joy stood on the ladder with her head inside, and watched the girls as they ran from one window to the next, ohing and ahing over the views.

Chase was too tall to stand, so he sat in one corner, his arm slung over his upturned knee. He caught Joy's eyes and winked. "I think they like it."

"I think you're right."

After a couple more minutes, Chase told the girls it was time to leave the fort. Kinsley cried, but Joy was able to take her out. Chase came down next with Harper, and they all stood on the ground.

"Now, what's the surprise?" Joy asked.

"It's in the barn." Chase still held Harper. "Boys, let's pick up the tools first and then head over to see the surprise."

Joy frowned, wondering what in the world he was so excited about. She'd been in the barn before. There was nothing but old tools, broken furniture and some potting supplies.

The boys picked up their hammers and a box of nails,

but other than that, they'd done a great job of keeping the space clean.

With their little brood around them, they walked along the service road to the barn. The boys couldn't talk about anything other than their fort, and the girls asked to go back.

Chase smiled at Joy from time to time, and she smiled back, thankful he'd helped the boys fulfill a dream.

When they reached the green barn, Chase led them inside and they set their tools on the workbench.

"Where's the surprise?" Ryan asked impatiently.

"It's upstairs in the old hayloft." Chase's eyes shone bright with anticipation. "Come on."

He took them through the potting shed, which connected the two ends of the barn, and into the eastern portion. An old carriage sat in the corner, long since forgotten.

"Wouldn't it be cool to pull out the carriage for the festival?" Chase asked.

She'd already contacted the automobile club, who had said they'd be happy to bring out their old cars—they'd probably love to see the carriage, too. "I think that's a great idea."

"Wait until you see what I found," Chase said as he led them up a narrow set of stairs. He still held Harper, who clapped with glee, though she probably had no idea what was happening.

"What did you find?" Jordan asked with wide eyes.

"Just wait."

Chase pushed open a door at the head of the stairs and everyone marched in behind him.

Joy had never been in the loft before. It was more like an attic, since it had a solid floor and slanted roof.

If Chase stood in the middle, he could stand straight, but if he moved to the right or left, he had to bend.

Two windows, one on either side, offered scant light for them to see. Chase reached over and flipped on a switch, revealing old electric lights. They hummed and hung on long wires.

The whole room became visible, but it took a moment for Joy's eyes to adjust.

Everywhere she looked were antiques—a spinning wheel, several trunks, a dressmaker's dummy, an oval mirror and more.

"I came up here the other day to look for the windows we used on the tree fort," Chase explained, his voice high with excitement. "And I found all this."

Joy and the kids followed him to the opposite side of the loft, and her eyes grew wide.

"It looks like someone in the Asher family hosted a carnival a long time ago and stored all the games up here."

"Whoa!" Ryan said as he knelt before a large clown face with a hole where the mouth should have been. "This is cool."

"I counted about ten games," Chase said, watching everyone's reaction. "There's a bowling set, a target game, a wheel of fortune, a ring toss and several others."

Joy could hardly believe what she was seeing: real antique carnival games.

"They need a little work," Chase said, "and maybe a touch of paint in a few places, but they are in excellent condition. I had Mr. Taylor come up here today to tell me how old he thought they might be and he said they are easily a hundred and twenty years old."

Joy touched the large target game. It stood as tall as her and was painted a bright yellow, which had faded with age. The details in the painting were exquisite. "Are you sure we should use them? Won't that devalue them?"

"They're worth more to us to use as games for our festival," Chase said. "My dad will just sell them with everything else, if he has a chance. Why not use them for what they were intended?"

It would save them time and money if they didn't have to build their own games for the festival.

"If Mrs. Thompson were here," Ryan said, "she'd say this is a blessing from God."

"And she'd be right," Chase agreed, ruffling Ryan's blond hair. "We needed games and God provided."

"Just like we needed a mom and God provided," Jordan added with a toothless grin.

Joy leaned down and kissed his nose. "And I needed some boys and God provided that, too."

"Now all we need is a forever dad and we'll have everything we need," Ryan said with a decisive nod.

Joy glanced up and found Chase watching her. The strong, steady look in his eyes made her cheeks grow warm.

"I think we should haul these outside and get a better look," she said quickly. "See what we're dealing with."

"I'll take the bowling pins!" Kodi said, gathering them in his short little arms.

The boys each grabbed something and started down the stairs.

"Ryan asked me about a forever dad a couple days ago," Chase said after the boys disappeared.

Joy still held Kinsley, so she looked down at her daughter and wiped an imaginary smudge off her cheek. "What did he say?"

"He said he wanted a dad like all the other kids—but he's worried that if you get married someday, your husband might not like him—or Ryan might not like your husband."

"That's a silly thing to worry about. I don't have any plans—"

"It's not silly to him."

She knew it was something to take seriously—and she'd talk to Ryan about it as soon as she had a chance—but she didn't want to encourage Chase to continue. "I'll talk to him."

Joy started to walk away, but Chase reached out and put his hand on her arm. "You're doing a great job, Joy, with everything. I'm sorry about the other night when Tom—"

"You don't need to apologize."

"But I want to." The sunshine filtered through the window, showing the dust flying through the air. "I want to make things easier for you—not harder."

She thought about the tree fort and the bank loan, and all the other ways Chase had helped, and she felt her face relaxing. "You are, and I'm thankful."

He smiled and it made her insides swirl with pleasure.

It was getting harder and harder to deny her feelings—and for some reason, that didn't scare her like it should.

Chapter Ten

It took them several weeks to prepare the carnival games among all their other responsibilities, but Chase had never enjoyed a project as much as he did when Joy and the kids helped him. They had cleaned, repaired and even painted a few of the games and they now stood waiting in the barn for the festival.

Word had traveled around town about the event and Joy had asked several people in church to come and offer tours. Chase and the boys had hung posters and Joy had been interviewed by the Timber Falls weekly newspaper, as well as the local radio station. Everyone was excited to see the mansion.

Among all their activities, Chase had started to attend services at Timber Falls Community Church with Joy and Mrs. Thompson, and he'd been there when Pastor Jacob had called for a special offering. They had been overwhelmed with the generosity of the congregants, and celebrated as Joy deposited another substantial check into her housing account.

But today, Chase had set aside all his other responsibilities, so he and the boys could work on a secret project just for Joy. They stood outside the barn in the chicken coop, the hot sun making the job more difficult and dirty. Sweat dripped down Chase's temples.

"Do you think she'll like it?" Jordan asked Chase, wrinkling his freckled nose.

"I think she'll love it," Chase told the little blond-haired boy. "I just hope it isn't too much work for her."

Ryan handed Chase a hammer and shrugged. "We'll help."

"And I'll help, too," Chase agreed—though he didn't know how long he'd stay at Bee Tree Hill once the sale was complete—whether that sale was to Joy or someone else. The thought of leaving Joy and the kids—and returning to his life in Seattle—felt like a knife turning in his chest. How would he ever go back to life as usual now that he was a dad?

The new chicken wire was easy enough to tack on to the original posts around the coop. He'd been happy to discover that the roost was in good condition. They'd simply cleaned out some of the debris left there over the years, fixed a post in the north corner of the coop and were now attaching new wire around the yard.

A half dozen Rhode Island Reds clucked from two crates stacked in the shade of the barn. He and the boys had purchased them from a local farmer's market just that morning. Chase didn't know much about keeping chickens, but he'd done a little research online and spent an hour with the farmer who sold him the birds. After the market, he and the boys visited the farming supply store and purchased the chicken wire, seed, a couple bales of fresh hay and a watering trough.

"She should be home in half an hour," Chase told the boys, "and I want it to be ready for her."

Kodi's face became serious and he nodded. "We'll get it done."

Chase smiled. The boys were so eager to learn, he loved teaching them. They were hard workers and took such pride in their work, Chase found himself coming up with projects they could help with, just to see them shine.

They finished securing the wire and spread hay in the roost. Ryan filled the watering trough and Jordan filled the feeder with seed. Chase asked Kodi to help him haul the crates over to the coop, and when the older boys were done with their chores, Chase carefully opened the first crate and tilted it so the birds would come out. They squawked and complained, and ran in several different directions. Thankfully, Chase had remembered to lock the gate. He opened the second crate and did the same.

The boys stood with Chase for several minutes watching the silly birds. It didn't take them long to find the water and seed and the boys laughed as they watched the birds peck at their food.

Chase's phone dinged and he pulled it out of his pocket. It was a text from Mrs. Thompson. Joy is home. I sent her and the girls to the barn. They'll be there in a minute.

"She's coming," Chase told the boys.

They scrambled to pick up the tools, their faces filled with excited anticipation.

Chase stacked the wooden crates in the corner of the coop and then called the boys to join him.

"Let's run into the barn and wash up quick." He led the way and they went to the small bathroom in the corner, where they washed their hands as quickly as possible.

"Hurry!" Ryan told his little brothers. "I see them coming!"

Anticipation mounted in Chase's chest, too, and he suddenly felt nervous. What if Joy thought the chickens

were a ridiculous gift? What if she didn't want them?
What if she took the gift the wrong way?

But what way did he want her to take the gift? Had he
done it simply as a thank-you for all the hard work she'd
been doing? Had he done it because he wanted to fulfill
a lifelong dream for her? Or had he done it because he
wanted her to be pleased with him?

He was still analyzing why he'd gone to all the trouble
when she appeared at the open barn door.

"What are you boys up to?" she asked with a curious smile.

Chase finished drying his hands on a paper towel and
tossed it into the garbage bin. He returned her smile, his
heart racing a little faster at seeing her. He didn't know
how it was possible, but she grew more and more beautiful each time he saw her. Today, she wore a medium-
length black skirt, which rippled when she walked, a
soft white T-shirt and a simple pair of sandals—but she
looked amazing.

"Chase!" Harper said as she ran across the length of
the barn and reached up to him. He scooped her into his
arms and held her close, his heart warming at her greeting. Joy hadn't told the girls—or the boys—about who
Chase really was yet, but he didn't mind. He knew she
was waiting for the right time. All that mattered right
now was that Chase knew.

"Mrs. Thompson told me you guys were busy today,"
Joy said, smoothing Ryan's hair. He'd also been sweating and his hair stuck up all over his head. "What have
you been working on?"

Ryan looked at Chase and said, "Can I tell her?"

"How about we show her, instead?" Chase asked.

The boys all agreed and jumped around Joy, unable

to contain their excitement. Ryan grabbed one hand and Kodi grabbed the other and they all left the barn.

Joy laughed at their enthusiasm and cast curious glances at Chase.

He followed close behind her with Harper and Kinsley in his arms.

When Joy rounded the corner, she stopped short.

"Surprise!" the boys shouted.

Chase came up beside her, a grin on his face. "We got you chickens."

The boys cheered and the girls squealed, wiggling out of Chase's arms to run to the coop, but Joy stood motionless.

Ryan ran with the other kids to the fence and they stood there, the boys excitedly telling Harper and Kinsley all about the chickens and everything they'd learned that day from the farmer.

"What do you think?" Chase asked Joy.

Her face was devoid of emotion as she stared at the coop.

Chase's excitement faded and he felt a rock settle in the pit of his stomach. "You don't like it."

She didn't say anything for a minute, but then finally swallowed. "Kids, it's time to wash up for supper. Mrs. Thompson has everything ready."

"Ah, Mom!" Ryan whined. "I want to stay with the chickens."

"I hold one?" Kinsley asked, her eyes shining.

"Not now." Joy took Kinsley and Harper by the hands. "We need to head back to the house."

"What's wrong?" Chase asked.

"Nothing." Joy didn't look at him as she motioned for the boys to follow her.

He moved to stand in front of her. "Did I do something wrong?"

"I don't want to talk about it." She took a deep breath, her lips trembling. "Please take the chickens back to where you bought them."

Ryan, Jordan and Kodi stood by Joy, their faces crestfallen.

Chase hated to see their disappointment. "We put a lot of work into the coop today—"

"I'm sorry, but I do not want them." She tried to smile at the boys. "Thank you—but we can't keep them."

Ryan's mouth hung open as he looked from Joy to Chase, "But Chase said—"

"Chase should have asked me first." She started to walk away.

Standing in the barnyard, Chase watched them leave, more disappointed than he should have been. It wasn't because he had put a lot of time and energy into the project—that didn't bother him—it was because he had thought she'd be just as excited as everyone else. But the reverse was true. She was upset—and he didn't know why.

Joy trembled from head to foot, her eyes burning with unshed tears as they crossed the back lawn.

"Why don't you like the chickens?" Ryan asked, trying to keep up with her pace. "We made the coop just for you."

Pain and guilt tightened her gut and she slowed her pace. "I'm sorry, Ry." Why was she being such a baby about this? She should have kept her reaction to herself, pretended to like Chase's gift—and then spoken to him privately about it when the kids weren't around.

"Do we have to get rid of them?" Jordan asked, his bottom lip quivering. "I like chickens."

"So do I," Kodi added.

"Me, too!" Kinsley said proudly.

Joy tried to take a deep breath to calm herself, but failed. "Chase had no right to make that decision for me. He should have asked before he bought the chickens."

"Isn't this his house?" Ryan asked.

"This is his house?" Jordan's eyes grew wide.

Now was not the time to explain the situation to the children—but Ryan was right, kind of. If Chase wanted chickens, who was she to stop him?

But he hadn't bought them for himself—he'd bought them for her—and that's what troubled her the most.

"You're right, Ryan. This is Chase's house. If he wants to keep the chickens," she paused to take control of her wobbling voice, "then I can't stop him."

"Joy," Chase called, jogging to catch up with them. "Can we talk?"

The last thing she wanted was to speak about this in front of the children.

"Ryan, I can see the kitchen door." She placed Harper's and Kinsley's hands into his. "Can you please take the girls and your brothers to Mrs. Thompson?"

Holding his mouth in a tight, disapproving line, Ryan walked everyone to the house.

Joy took a deep breath and turned to face Chase.

He stood before her in a pair of blue jeans and a light button-down shirt tucked in at his waist. He'd rolled up the sleeves and left the top buttons undone. It was evident he'd been working hard.

"I don't understand what went wrong," he said.

Joy glanced over her shoulder and saw the kids entering the kitchen, so she let out a breath. "Why did you get me chickens?"

He frowned. "I thought you always wanted them."

"But why chickens?"

Chase lifted his hands in confusion. "Just the other night, you said—"

"No." She crossed her arms, almost as a way to protect herself—to protect her heart. "I know I said I always wanted chickens—but why did you give them to me—why something so personal?"

"Chickens are personal?" He frowned.

"They are when I've always wanted them, and when they're connected to one of the only good memories I have of my mother." She finally gained control of her voice, but just barely. "And when you knew how important that dream was, you still gave them to me."

"They're a gift—that's all."

She shook her head. "What are we doing, Chase?" She motioned to where the children had just gone. "I appreciate that you're hanging out with the boys, teaching them things I could never teach them—but ultimately, you're going to go back to Seattle—right? What good is it to build a chicken coop and buy me chickens when you're leaving, and I might be leaving, too?"

A swinging bench hung from a large branch on a nearby oak. Chase ran his hand through his hair and walked over to the swing. He sat, looking out at the river.

Joy sighed and walked over to join him.

They sat side by side and pushed the swing back and forth for a little while before he answered. "I don't know what to tell you, Joy. A few weeks ago, when I arrived, I thought this would be a quiet, easy transition. I knew exactly what I was doing and why I was doing it—but now—" He leaned his head back and let out a frustrated breath. "Now I don't know what I'm doing."

A flock of ducks took flight from the river, squawking and flapping their wings. Water dropped from their bodies like thousands of little sparkling pebbles, dimpling the surface of the Mississippi.

"I'm sorry about my reaction to the chickens," she said. "I know you and the boys worked hard to give me that gift—but, Chase, I can't take gifts like that from you. It's too personal—too permanent."

Her hand lay on the bench between them and Chase looked down at it. "What if I wanted it to be personal?" he asked quietly.

Joy's heart raced and her breath caught. He started to move his hand to cover hers, so she stood, making the swing lurch to a halt.

She faced Chase, anger, sadness, disappointment and grief warring within her. Her heart was softening toward him, but she couldn't let it. Even if he was a good man— even if he was kind and patient with the kids—even if he was the father of her daughters—she couldn't risk him making the same choice as before. If something threatened him, or he was forced to choose between his father and her, how could she be certain he'd choose her? He hadn't last time—why would he now?

"It can't be personal," she said, shaking her head. "And it can't be permanent. When the sale of Bee Tree Hill is complete, I want you to go back to your life—I need you to go back." She tried to keep the tears from gathering in her eyes, but it was pointless. "I will never keep the girls from you—you're welcome to come see them whenever you'd like. I'll send pictures and we can video chat when you're away—but that's all. I don't have space in my life for anything more than that."

He watched her as she spoke, his face betraying his disappointment. "But what if I don't want to leave? What if video chats and occasional visits aren't enough for me?" He stood and walked to her. "What if I want to see my girls every day? What if I want to be a part of their lives—help you make decisions—teach them and guide them?"

"W-what are you saying, Chase?" She wiped at the tears, her pulse thrumming in her wrists. "Are you saying you'll give up your life in Seattle and move to Timber Falls? What will you do for a living? All you know is the Asher Corporation—it's your legacy."

"It's the girls' legacy, too."

"Yes—but the Ashers are done here in Timber Falls. Your life is in Seattle, your work is in Seattle—the only thing here is us."

He stepped closer to her. "What if that's enough?"

She shook her head. "It won't be enough for you—I know that firsthand."

He closed his eyes briefly and sighed.

"I can't tell you where to live or how to live," she said, "but I can tell you that there is no room in my life for us." She motioned between her and Chase, not even sure if he wanted an "us," but needing him to know where she stood.

He didn't say anything for a few heartbeats. "I know I hurt you, Joy, and I wish you knew how sorry I am." He paused and looked at the river to compose his emotions. When he met her gaze again, he said, "You're right. My life and work are in Seattle, but now my heart is here in Timber Falls. I care about you and the kids more than you know. I'm not sure what the future holds for me—but I know I cannot go back to the life I was living. Please be patient with me as I figure out what to do next."

It was a simple, yet complicated request. The least she could do was be patient with him.

"I will." She nodded. "But, please, as you're trying to figure things out, know that I cannot be a part of that future."

Joy had nothing left to say, so she walked past him toward the house.

She knew she had done the right thing and made the right decision, so then why did she feel like she'd just made a huge mistake? Hadn't she dreamed Chase would realize his mistake and come back for her? Today was the first indication that he still cared about her and she had reacted so poorly.

Forcing her thoughts to quiet, she continued toward the house, praying to find a way to purchase Bee Tree Hill as soon as possible so Chase could go back to Seattle.

Chapter Eleven

Chase returned to the swing and sat there for a long time, his head in his hands. How could a few chickens cause so much turmoil?

If he was honest, he knew this had nothing to do with the chickens, and everything to do with Joy's hurt and fears. He had found the one gift that would mean the most to her and show her how much he cared. It scared her. He got that—he just hadn't expected it to make her so upset.

His phone rang and he pulled it from his back pocket.

It was his dad.

Malcolm Asher was the last person Chase wanted to talk to right now, so he turned off the ringer and put his phone back.

The sun set and the lights in the main house turned on. Mosquitoes started to bite and he swatted at them, irritated by their annoying buzz.

No doubt Mrs. Thompson had already served supper, but Chase would have to eat alone tonight. He couldn't walk into that house and face Joy right now.

When she told him that there was no future for them, something had twisted in his gut. He had left her four years ago, and it had hurt her, but he realized in that moment that he'd always hoped there was a way to fix things, to somehow return to where they had once been.

But now that he knew there wasn't, he wanted it more than ever. He loved Joy, had never stopped, and seeing her as a strong, independent and patient mom had only strengthened those feelings.

No matter how she felt about him, though, it didn't change his desire to help her and the kids.

He stood and walked toward the carriage house. His stomach growled, but he'd have to settle for cereal. Mrs. Thompson would go out of her way to reheat some leftovers if he went to the main house right now, but he wouldn't do that to Joy. She probably wanted him to stay away tonight.

The carriage house was dark, so he switched on the light when he entered. Everything was as he left it—empty and cold. His thoughts wandered up the hill to the main house where the kids were probably playing a game or watching a movie. Joy would be getting the girls ready for bed. Harper would want a story read to her and Kinsley would be talking about all the things they had done that day. No doubt she would be asking all sorts of questions about the chickens, reminding Joy of the awkward moment when he had suggested they were meant as a personal gift.

He closed the door and went to the cupboard to get out the cereal and a bowl, but he just stood there for a minute, berating himself for being so clumsy with Joy.

A ping sounded from his phone, so he pulled it out to look at the text.

Listen to my message. His dad again.

Chase pulled a chair out from the table and sat. He tapped the voice mail icon and put the phone to his ear.

I just spoke to Tidwell and he told me you won't show him the property until August. Dad's voice was deep and painfully steady. *You're trying my patience, Chase. You*

have exactly two hours to call Tidwell and schedule an
appointment to show him Bee Tree Hill at his earliest
convenience. This is your last warning.

The message ended.

Chase set the phone on the top of the table and leaned
back in his chair, running his hands through his hair.
It was only the first of July. They still had almost four
weeks until the festival, and Mr. Taylor was only halfway
through his work. He had just told Chase yesterday that
he needed at least two more weeks to finish his inventory and make a final assessment. Mr. Taylor had also
recommended a historical property specialist from Saint
Paul who would be arriving in the morning. He and Mr.
Taylor would discuss Bee Tree Hill and the specialist
would give Chase a property value.

He'd finally know exactly what the property was
worth and how much he and Joy would need to scrape
together to buy the place from the Asher Corporation.

"Lord," Chase said into the quiet house, closing his
eyes and dipping his head, "all this feels impossible to
me right now, but Your word says that nothing is impossible for You. I know my father and I know what happens when he gets his mind set. I pray You would make
a way for me to give this home to Joy and the kids. Help
me to make the right decisions, say the right things and
do what I need to do to save the property from an investor." He let out a low, steady breath, feeling a little more
peaceful leaving this problem in God's hands. "And if
it's not Your will, please show me what You want me to
do. Help me be the dad I need to be, and help me heal the
hurt I caused Joy. In Your name, I pray. Amen."

It wasn't an eloquent prayer, but it was heartfelt and
it was all Chase could think to do.

When he opened his eyes, he picked up his phone

and found Conrad Tidwell's number in his contacts. He pressed Call and waited as the phone rang.

"Hello, Chase," Mr. Tidwell said. "I was hoping you'd call me back."

"Hello, Mr. Tidwell." Chase stood and paced over to the window, which looked out at the pond. The sky was already dark, but it wasn't hard to imagine what the pond looked like in his mind's eye. He braced himself, knowing he had little choice. "When would you like to see the property?"

"I am planning to fly into Minneapolis on the morning of July twenty-eighth. I can be in Timber Falls by noon."

It would be the day after the festival. At least they could still hold that as planned.

"I can make the twenty-eighth work." Chase shoved his free hand into his pocket. "I should have all the property assessments ready by that time."

"Good. I'm eager to see the estate." Mr. Tidwell sounded pleased. "I will be there on the twenty-eighth."

"If you have any questions before then, don't hesitate to call or text."

"I will. Thank you."

"We'll see you on the twenty-eighth at noon."

"Goodbye."

Chase tapped the red phone icon and stared at the home screen for a minute. He hated that he didn't have more time—but he was thankful for the time he'd been given.

At least there were four more weeks until Tidwell showed up. Chase would use those four weeks to fight for more than the house. He was ready to fight for Joy and the kids, too.

"Thank you," Joy said to Mr. Johnson at the movie theater the next afternoon as she stood near the ticket counter.

The smell of fresh popcorn wafted through the air, making her stomach growl. She'd been out collecting donations all morning and hadn't stopped to eat lunch. "I appreciate the donation and I hope to see you at the festival."

"You can count on it, Joy." Mr. Johnson was a tall man with gray hair and thick glasses. "Mary and I wouldn't miss it for the world."

She picked up the basket he'd put together for the silent auction they would hold during the Bee Tree Hill Festival. The basket held a ten-pack of tickets, a popcorn bucket full of coupons for free popcorn and half a dozen boxes of theater candy.

Pushing open the door, she stepped onto the sidewalk running along Main Street and paused when she saw Chase's red Jeep parked near her minivan.

He leaned against the front fender wearing a navy blue polo shirt, a pair of khaki shorts and brown flip-flops. Sunglasses hid his eyes, but they did not hide the dazzling smile he gave her.

Nerves bubbled in her chest and she had to catch her breath. Despite her best efforts, he still made her heart pound.

"Mrs. Thompson told me where I could find you." He pushed away from the Jeep and walked over to her. Without asking, he took the basket out of her hands and went to the minivan.

Joy clicked the unlock button on her key fob. Chase opened the back gate and set the basket next to the others.

"What are you doing downtown?" she finally managed to ask.

They hadn't spoken since the night before when she'd overreacted about the chickens. That morning, she'd left before he came to the house for breakfast and she thought he'd be busy with the property assessor for the rest of the day.

"I wanted to help you," he said while closing the back gate.

"I think I'm done for the day." She had spent all morning downtown going from shop to shop asking for donations. It was a humbling experience, but she was doing it for the kids—and not one single person had said no. They knew Joy, whether from church, from her work at the elementary school or from just growing up in the community. They also loved Bee Tree Hill and wanted it to be owned by a local family. News traveled fast and everyone knew the Asher Corporation planned to sell the property.

"That's even better," Chase said. "I was hoping to take you out to lunch. I have a feeling you didn't stop to eat."

"Am I that predictable?"

"Yes."

She smiled, but then her smile faded and she said, "I don't know, Chase."

His eyes were shaded by his sunglasses as he regarded her. "I'm sorry about last night—"

"I'm the one who should apologize."

"No." He shook his head. "I haven't been handling any of this well."

"You've been amazing. You're so good with the kids."

"But I want to be good with you, too." He took off his sunglasses and his blue eyes were bright with apology. "I want to be friends, Joy—if for no other reason than because of Harper and Kinsley."

He was right. They would forever share their daughters. No matter how much she wanted distance to protect her heart, he would always be a part of her life. Friendship would make that a lot easier.

"I want to take you out to eat as a friend and nothing

more." His eyes softened and he smiled. "I like you and I want you to like me again, too."

She did like him—more than she should. "I don't think it'll be hard to become friends."

His smile was warm, but a shadow passed over his eyes. "That's the best thing I've heard all day."

"Did you speak to the assessor?"

He put his glasses back on and tilted his head. "Let me buy you lunch and I'll tell you all about it."

She locked the minivan doors and walked to the end of the street with him. They waited at the stoplight and then took the crosswalk to the other side of Main Street. The ash trees lining the street were in full bloom, their green leaves shading the historic streetlights and lush planters. Pink-and-white impatiens overgrew their containers, dripping around the edges, intermixing with the trailing ivy.

A gentle breeze ruffled Joy's hair as Chase led her into Ruby's Bistro. The owner, Ruby Farrow, had moved to Timber Falls from the Twin Cities a dozen years before and renovated an old hardware store into an upscale restaurant. She was a Le Cordon Bleu chef and offered an array of culinary items not seen anywhere else in Timber Falls. It was Joy's favorite place to eat—other than Mrs. Thompson's kitchen.

They were shown to a small table near one of the large plateglass windows near the front of the building and given menus.

After their orders were placed, Joy leaned back in her chair and studied Chase. "What happened at the house today?"

He took a sip of his water and set down his glass. His sunglasses were on the table and he began to fiddle with them. "I took Mr. O'Conner through the property, answered all his questions and then gave him and

Mr. Taylor some time to confer." He looked up from his sunglasses and met her gaze. "He valued the property at slightly higher than I had hoped."

In most other situations, an owner would be happy to hear their property was worth more than they had thought—but not this time. Joy nibbled her bottom lip and tried not to let her disappointment show.

"Don't worry," he said. "With the last two grants you were awarded, the loan I qualified for and all the donations you've been given, we're almost halfway to our goal."

She tried to feel hopeful, but they only had a few more weeks.

"Mr. Asher?" An older woman approached their table.

Joy recognized her as Marcy Hanover. She didn't know her personally, but Marcy had written for the Timber Falls weekly newspaper years ago. She was probably seventy now, but she was still healthy and active. Even though she didn't write anymore, she still volunteered for several service organizations and at the county historical society.

"Are you Chase Asher?" Marcy asked.

Chase stood and extended his hand. "I am."

Marcy shook his hand, her eyes wide. "I'm Marcy Hanover. Your uncle Morgan and I used to be very close."

Joy frowned. Uncle Morgan had never mentioned a relationship with Marcy—but now that she thought about it, Morgan always attended the yearly historical society members meeting, regularly attended the monthly Exchange Club meetings that Marcy presided over, gave generously to the downtown-beautification organization that Marcy spearheaded and was responsible for the beautiful flower planters outside.

Maybe Morgan and Marcy were sweethearts once upon a time—but if they had been, what happened?

"It's a pleasure to meet you," Chase said.

Marcy turned to wave over a table full of elderly ladies who had been sitting in the corner. They stood and came toward Chase and Joy with schoolgirl giggles and bright eyes. Each one was older than Mrs. Thompson, and some were more bent than others, but they looked at Chase like he was a celebrity.

"I told you this was Chase Asher," Marcy said to her retinue.

"Isn't he a handsome young man?" one of the ladies said, as if Chase wasn't standing three feet in front of her.

"My, yes," said another with a grin.

"And look at those eyes," said a third. "Have you ever seen such blue eyes?"

"If I was fifty years younger, he wouldn't have a chance," said another.

The whole group laughed at that statement.

"Ladies," Chase said, an embarrassed smile on his face. "It's nice to meet all of you—"

"And he's a millionaire," said a different woman with bright red lipstick. "Handsome and rich."

"My father is the millionaire—"

"Joy." One of the women in the back stepped forward and Joy recognized her from church. "Are you and Mr. Asher a couple?"

Chase turned to Joy, an apologetic look on his face.

"No," Joy said, shaking her head. "We're just *friends*."

He smiled at her.

"I wouldn't mind being his friend," the oldest woman in the group said with a sigh.

Chase sent Joy a pleading look, but she could only smile and watch.

"We were wondering if you'd do us a favor," Marcy said to Chase.

His cheeks had colored from all their attention, but he handled it so well, Joy could only marvel. "Of course," he said.

The group twittered with excitement.

"We heard about the Bee Tree Hill Festival," Marcy said. "And we also heard that Miss Gordon was asking service organizations in town to make donations to the event."

Joy sat at the table, but Marcy didn't address her.

"You've heard correct." Chase was respectful and sweet, even though she could tell he was uncomfortable with all the attention.

"Good." Marcy turned to the other ladies and they all nodded their encouragement to continue. "Because we have an idea for the auction."

"I'm excited to hear your idea," Chase said.

Marcy took a deep breath. The wrinkles around her eyes deepened as she smiled. "We want you to auction off yourself."

The smile on Chase's face fell away. "Excuse me?"

"Like an old-fashioned bachelor auction," Marcy said. "We'll all bid on a date with you."

"It'll all be innocent and in good fun, of course," said the lady from Joy's church.

Joy had to put her hand up to hide her smile.

"We just want a chance to relive our youth for an afternoon," said another.

"You want to bid on a date—with me?" Chase frowned.

"You're the most eligible bachelor in town," Marcy said and the others nodded in agreement. "We think you'll fetch a handsome sum of money for Miss Gordon's cause."

"Most definitely," said the oldest lady.

Chase glanced at Joy, a mixture of horror and honor on his face.

Joy bit her lips so she wouldn't giggle.

"Think of the children," said Marcy, her face serious. The other women all nodded.

"Miss Gordon has done so much for those little boys," Marcy continued. "We all want to help and we agree this is the best use of our money."

This time, when Chase looked at Joy with a question in his eyes, she shrugged. "It's for the children," she said.

Chase ran his hand through his hair and rested it on the back of his neck as he squinted for a moment. "I suppose, if it's for the children, how could I say no?"

"Oh, good!" Marcy and the others clapped and voiced their pleasure.

Marcy finally turned and acknowledged Joy. "Be sure to organize all the details, Miss Gordon, and I'll be sure to bring my checkbook."

"I will," Joy said.

"We'll let you two get back to your lunch." Marcy gathered the women together like a flock of wandering ducklings and they went back to their table, giggling and chatting the whole way. Several cast appreciative glances back in Chase's direction.

Chase slowly sat, an embarrased flush in his cheeks. "What just happened?"

Joy started to laugh and she couldn't speak for a moment.

"It's not funny," he said, trying to suppress the laughter in his voice. "No one even knows my name in my apartment building in Seattle—but here—"

"In a small town, everyone knows who you are."

"Do you ever get used to it?" Chase asked.

She shrugged. "I've never lived anywhere else." Joy

readjusted her silverware and lined it on the table. "Unfortunately, it's taken me most of my adult life to lose the stigma of being a foster child—the kid abandoned and left alone for over a month."

He grew serious. "Have you ever wanted to leave Timber Falls?"

"I planned to leave as soon as I finished college." She couldn't look him in the eyes. "But my life took a turn I didn't expect."

"I'm sorry, Joy." He reached across the table and set his hand over hers.

His touch was soft and gentle, and full of such tenderness, she had to swallow the unexpected emotions clogging her throat.

"You need to stop apologizing," she said, meeting his gaze. "I'm happy I stayed. I made choices, too."

"But I left."

"And I chose not to tell you the truth sooner."

Pulling his hand away, he offered a half smile. "Do you think we could start over?"

Could they? "I guess there's no way to know unless we try."

"I'd like that."

"So would I."

Their waitress appeared with their meals and Joy was thankful for the distraction. She didn't want to talk about the past anymore. She was ready to start discussing the future—whatever that might be.

Chapter Twelve

Sunshine rippled across the water as Chase reclined on the red-and-white-checkered blanket they'd set out for their Fourth of July picnic. A huge oak tree unfurled its ancient branches overhead, providing the perfect amount of shade. The delicious meal of fried chicken, potato salad and chocolate cake that Mrs. Thompson and Joy had prepared was eaten and the leftovers were stored in the cooler.

"We go swimming?" Kinsley asked as Joy applied more sunscreen to Kinsley's nose.

"Not today. The river is too high." Joy had to move fast to get the sunscreen on Kinny's face.

"Will there be fireworks tonight?" Jordan asked, sitting on the blanket next to Joy.

"They will shoot them off from the park across the river," Joy answered patiently for the tenth time that day. "When the sun goes down."

"Will we be awake then?" Ryan asked.

"I'll be sure to keep you awake," Mrs. Thompson answered and winked at Chase.

Chase winked back, but Joy was so busy slathering sunscreen on the kids, she didn't notice.

"Can we play in the tree fort now?" Kodi asked.

Joy stopped fighting Kinsley and wiped her hands on the corner of the cloth. "Sure."

The boys didn't waste a minute. They took off for the tree fort without looking back.

"I think I'll bring the food up to the kitchen and put it in the refrigerator," Mrs. Thompson said.

"I'll help." Joy started to stand, but Mrs. Thompson shook her head.

"Stay here and enjoy yourself for a bit." Mrs. Thompson tried to get off the blanket, but struggled, so Chase jumped up and gave her a hand. "Thanks, honey," she said.

The cooler was in the boys' wagon, so she picked up the handle and started toward the service road leading up to the house.

Harper sat on the blanket with her feet stuck out in front of her, a book in her lap, like usual.

"I throw sticks in the water?" Kinsley asked.

Joy shook her head. "Why don't you stay here and I'll read to you and Harper."

Chase sat on the blanket again, watching Joy and the girls. He still marveled that they were his daughters.

Harper stood and walked across the blanket. She stopped in front of Chase and smiled, her brown eyes sparkling. "You read to me?" She extended her book.

Chase glanced at Joy. "Do you mind?"

She smiled and shook her head. "Of course not."

Kinsley came over and also sat in Chase's lap. The girls snuggled close to him, and he hugged them before he opened the book.

Joy lay on her side, her hand supporting her head as she watched him read. Once in a while, he glanced at her to see if she'd fallen asleep, but she was wide awake, the expression on her face unreadable.

The story was another favorite of Harper's. It was about a scared little llama that was afraid of the dark.

When he came to the end, he closed the book and looked down at the girls. Their eyelids were heavy, but neither one had fallen asleep.

"Chase?" Joy asked quietly.

He met her gaze.

"Is it alright if I tell the girls?"

His heart started to pound and he swallowed the rush of unexpected nerves. Was she ready to tell Harper and Kinsley he was their father? Once she did, there was no going back—for any of them. But he couldn't think of anything he wanted more.

Everything would change—forever. No longer would he be a stranger. He'd be their dad, with every responsibility and privilege that came with that honor.

He nodded. "Yes."

"What, Mama?" Kinsley asked.

Joy sat up and moved across the blanket to sit in front of Chase. Harper reached for her and she took the little girl into her lap. She cuddled her close and then looked between both of their girls.

"I thought it was time to tell you something very important."

"What, Mama?" Kinsley asked again.

"Chase is your daddy."

Kinsley and Harper both looked up at him. Their identical brown eyes stared at him in curiosity.

"My daddy?" Kinsley asked him.

He couldn't find his voice, so he simply nodded.

Without hesitation, she smiled at him and everything

else faded away. She leaned into him and said with a sigh, "My daddy."

Warmth filled Chase's chest and he tried to hold on to the moment as he held the little girl close.

Harper watched him in her quiet, gentle way. It wasn't uncertainty he saw in her eyes, but hesitation. After a moment, she looked up at Joy with a question in her eyes.

Joy simply nodded, as if she knew what their daughter was asking.

At her mother's reassurance, Harper's lips turned up into the most amazing smile Chase had ever seen in his life. Her eyes danced and her little shoulders came up in excitement—but she didn't voice her pleasure or even leave her mother's lap to hug Chase.

Instead, she stayed where she was and continued to smile.

"Your name is Daddy?" Kinsley asked Chase.

He looked at Joy for her approval.

She met his question with a smile of her own. "Do you want them to call you Daddy?"

"I do." More than he realized until that very moment.

"Yes," Joy said to Kinsley. "His name is Daddy."

Kinsley burrowed deeper into his arms and yawned. "I love you, Daddy."

Tears burned the backs of Chase's eyes for the first time in years. "I love you, too, Kinney." He met Harper's gaze. "And I love you, Harper."

The first blush of bashfulness came over Harper as she turned her cheek against Joy's chest—a smile still on her lips.

"I think it's time for a nap," Joy said to the girls, wiping at her cheeks. "We've all had a busy day."

Joy stood with Harper in her arms and Chase followed.

They didn't speak as they left the blanket and started to walk toward the house.

After a few moments, Chase looked at Joy over Kinsley's head and said, "Thank you."

She nodded.

They passed the boys and Joy told them to be careful in the tree house, then they continued up to the kitchen door.

No doubt the boys would have questions when they heard Harper and Kinsley calling him Daddy, but he and Joy would deal with that when the time came.

Mrs. Thompson was in the kitchen humming to herself as she ran a wet rag over the counters. She smiled at them when they entered.

"Chase is my daddy," Kinsley said to Mrs. Thompson.

Chase paused in his tracks and met the stunned expression on Mrs. Thompson's face. To her credit, she quickly recovered. "I know that, sweetie."

Kinsley hugged Chase's neck even tighter.

He laughed, and in that moment he knew without a doubt that he could never walk away from these girls. In a few short weeks, they had become his world.

Joy led the way up the stairs and laid Harper on her bed. The little girl sought out Chase's gaze one more time before she smiled and closed her eyes.

Kinsley wasn't as easy to get to sleep. When Chase set her on her bed, she sat there and grinned at him.

"It's time for your nap," Joy said, bringing a blanket over from the chair and spreading it across Kinsley's legs.

Kinsley lay down and wiggled in excitement.

Joy had to settle the blankets over her again and put her hand on Kinsley's forehead. "Sleep tight, little one."

Kinsley blinked several times and yawned.

Joy walked to the door and motioned for Chase to follow her out.

She closed the door behind him and stood in the semidark hallway. "I'm sorry for springing that on you."

Chase shook his head. "I'm happy you did."

"I should have given you more time to decide."

"I would have said yes, no matter how much time you gave me."

"But now you're committed."

He didn't hesitate. "I made the decision to be committed the moment you told me I was their father."

She studied him. "Are you sure?"

"More sure than I've ever been in my life."

Joy moistened her lips and nodded her head slowly. "Okay."

He smiled. "I'm happy they know."

She was quiet for a moment, but then she returned his smile. "So am I."

"I have a surprise for you, too." He moved away from the girls' door and into the main part of the hallway.

Frowning, she followed him. "What?"

"Mrs. Thompson agreed to babysit the children tonight so I could take you somewhere special."

Her frown deepened with curiosity. "Where?"

"It's a surprise."

"But what about the fireworks?"

"Mrs. Thompson will take the kids outside to watch the fireworks and then she'll put them all in bed for us."

"But—"

"Just say yes," he said. "I want to take you somewhere this evening and I don't want you to say no."

Her chest expanded with a deep breath—when she let it out, she said, "This isn't a date."

He shook his head. "It's not a date."

"We're going as friends."

"Just friends."

She bit her bottom lip.

"Will you say yes?" he asked.

"Yes." She put her hands up to her cheeks and smiled.

He smiled, too. He couldn't wait to take her out and have a little time alone.

Chase was determined to prove to Joy that he was a man worthy of her love—and he'd start tonight.

Pink, purple and orange spread across the western horizon as Chase led Joy out of the main gate of Bee Tree Hill. The air had already started to cool, making her happy she'd brought along a light sweater, which she pulled onto her arms. She'd changed into a summer dress and put on heeled sandals. She'd even taken the time to curl her hair and put on some fresh makeup before joining Chase in the foyer.

And she was happy she had, because he'd gone to the carriage house and changed into a pair of dark blue jeans, a button-down shirt and a dark suit jacket. His eyes had been bright when he saw her coming down the stairs and her cheeks were still warm from the memory.

Now, as she walked beside him, she felt like she had over four years ago when he'd taken her out on their first date.

But this wasn't a date—at least, that's what she kept telling herself.

Because it felt an awful lot like a date.

"You look really pretty tonight," he said.

"Thank you." She wanted to tell him he looked amazing, too, but she couldn't find the words.

They walked along the fence hugging the front of the Ashers' property. Cars were parked along Main Street and people were heading in the general direction that Joy and Chase were heading.

"Are we going to the Fourth of July celebration in the park?" she asked, almost certain they were.

"I heard there is dancing."

Their hands brushed together as they walked and a thrill raced up Joy's arm.

"Do you like to dance?" he asked.

"I love it."

His hand brushed hers again, and this time, she suspected that it wasn't an accident.

Since the park hugged the opposite side of the pond connecting it to Bee Tree Hill property, they didn't have far to walk.

The city park had several fountains springing forth from ponds, a large pavilion that housed the dancing, and meandering paths that wove in and out of willow trees along the riverbanks. Main Street sat high above the park and they had to descend a couple flights of stairs.

Hundreds of people had gathered to enjoy the celebration. The live orchestra played under the pavilion, their beautiful music floating on the gentle breeze, beckoning Chase and Joy to join in the fun.

"What will people think when they see us together?" Joy asked.

"Whatever they want." Chase took her hand and slipped it inside his elbow. "Are you afraid of what they might think?"

Her heart skipped a beat at his touch, but she didn't pull away. She loved the feel of being close to him. It brought back a summertime of memories—and this time, they were all good.

"I suppose they'll learn the truth about the girls eventually." They walked so close together, she had to look up at him to meet his gaze. "Does that bother you?"

"I couldn't be more proud to be known as their father."

Her heart expanded at his words and she smiled.

They walked along a path that led them over a foot-bridge, past the fountains and into the pavilion. It sat close to the water and offered a perfect view of the magnificent waterfalls, which gave Timber Falls its name. The waterfalls had attracted Chase's ancestors to choose this place to build their large sawmill in the 1890s, and it was the abundance of timber in the area that had inspired the name.

Strings of white lights dipped from the corners of the pavilion and met in the middle. They sparkled and swayed in the breeze. Joy knew dozens of people who had gathered, but she hardly noticed anyone as Chase took her hand and walked her onto the dance floor.

The orchestra played "The Way You Look Tonight," the stringed instruments humming with the beautiful song. The sound filled the space and wrapped around Joy as Chase turned to face her.

"May I have this dance?" he asked.

She nodded and stepped into his arms. He put his right hand on the small of her back and she had to remember to breathe. She put her left hand on his shoulder, and then they clasped their free hands. They stood close—closer than necessary, but she didn't want to move away.

He was a graceful dancer and he waltzed her around the dance floor with more experience than she had expected. She had taken a ballroom-dancing class in college for her physical-education credit and she was happy she had paid attention. It wasn't hard to let him lead her—he was strong and athletic, but his movements were smooth and easy to follow.

Everything else faded away as she danced with Chase. He smiled down at her and she felt more beautiful than ever. She didn't know how he did it, but he made her feel like there was no one else in the world and he only had eyes for her. It was a heady feeling and she forced herself to remember that this was *not* a date—yet she'd never felt this way in the presence of a friend before.

They danced through three songs, and when the third song ended, the orchestra conductor announced that they would take a break for the fireworks.

"Should we find somewhere to sit?" Chase asked, indicating the riverbank.

They left the pavilion and walked down the crushed-gravel path, taking their time finding a spot. The willow trees were the only hindrance to their view of the fireworks. Here and there, people were already sitting, so it took them a few minutes to find just the right place.

"How does this look?" Chase asked, finding a spot near one of the willows. The branches opened up just enough to give them a clear view across the river.

"Perfect."

"Here." Chase took off his jacket and set it on the ground.

"You want me to sit on your jacket?"

He smiled. "Isn't it gallant of me?"

She smiled and nodded. "Very."

After she sat, he joined her, sitting closer than she had expected.

Again, she didn't pull away. It felt good having his attention—and seeing the curious eyes of her friends and neighbors as they passed by.

Quiet conversation hummed around them. Even though there were people close by, somehow it felt like they were alone.

"I'm having a good time," she said softly.

The breeze made the long hanging willow branches sway all around as he turned to look at her. "Me, too," he said just as softly.

He smelled of cologne and fresh laundry soap. He was so close, their shoulders brushed.

"Are you sure this isn't a date?" she asked, her attention caught on his lips.

It took him a moment to answer. His chest rose and fell a few times. "I'm not sure anymore." His gaze moved to her mouth. "Do you want it to be a date?"

Every nerve in her body came alive and hummed with anticipation. What was she doing? Hadn't she warned herself not to fall in love with Chase again? But there was something about him—the same qualities that had made her fall hard last time were now more prominent than before. And this time, he was the father of her twins—the handsome, kind and selfless man who would forever and always be Harper and Kinsley's daddy.

"Chase," she whispered as she leaned closer, "I—"

Several bangs ripped through the air and the dark sky filled with the light of colorful fireworks.

Joy tore her focus from Chase and took a deep, shuddering breath.

She had almost kissed him—despite all the doubts and fears that still plagued her.

Chase reached through the dark and took her hand in his.

Catching her breath, she allowed him to run his thumb over the back of her hand. She tried to focus on the fireworks, but she couldn't see past the sensations tingling up her arms.

But as the fireworks continued, each bang felt more and more like a fist to her chest. Memories started to assail her, unwanted and unwelcomed. The banging of the front door as her mom walked out and left her alone, the banging of the fists against flesh in the first foster home she lived in, the banging voices of countless children mocking her in school, making her feel worthless—and the banging of car doors as boyfriends broke up with her when they learned who she was.

But the worst memory was the one where Chase's father had made her feel inferior and dirty—and then she'd been forced to listen to the front door bang again—and the car door bang again—as Chase left, knowing he'd finally realized it, too.

How long until he remembered why he'd left her the first time? How long until his father showed up and belittled her again? How long until Chase walked away, like so many others in her life? Because it wasn't a matter of if—but when.

Suddenly feeling cold and shaky, she pulled her hand away from his.

He turned questioning eyes to her. "What's wrong?"

Joy wrapped her arms around herself and tried not to feel ill. The fireworks shot up into the sky, one after the other, while the crowd oohed and aahed. "I can't do this," she whispered.

Chase leaned closer. "You can't what?"

"I can't do this," she said a little louder.

He sat back and nodded, understanding and empathy in his eyes—but his compassion only made her more upset. Why did he continue to be so good and kind to her when she was a mess?

Anger started to build inside her chest—but it wasn't anger at him, it was anger at herself. Why couldn't she be a normal person who could put her trust in people? Why did she always expect the worst? Yes, some people had proven that they couldn't be trusted—but there were others like Morgan Asher and Mrs. Thompson, who had shown her what true, unconditional love looked like. Why didn't she think Chase could do the same?

She wanted to lean into him again—throw all caution to the wind—but life had taught her to protect herself at all costs, and keeping her distance from Chase was the only way to do that.

"I'm sorry," she said, shaking her head.

"It's okay, Joy." He touched her cheek with his thumb and moved a piece of hair off her face. "I'm not going anywhere. We don't need to rush."

She closed her eyes at the feel of his hand and leaned into it.

The fireworks continued to boom over the river and she forced herself to take a deep, steady breath.

When she opened her eyes again, Chase offered her a slow, promising smile.

He was still beside her—but for how long, she didn't know.

Chapter Thirteen

Joy hummed as she ran the vacuum cleaner over the carpet in the master bedroom. Her arm was sore from the thousands of square feet she had already vacuumed that morning, but her heart was light. A half-dozen women had shown up that morning from church to help clean and prepare the house for the festival the following day. The same women would return tomorrow and help give tours of the mansion in period clothing they had rented from a costume shop.

All week, Joy, Mrs. Thompson, Chase and the kids had worked on the festival preparations. They had cleaned, cooked and cleaned some more. Today they would do last-minute chores like vacuuming, dusting, food preparation and various other tasks.

Joy would be up way past her bedtime in order to get everything ready, but she didn't mind. Chase would be by her side.

Outside, Chase and several men from church were mowing, weed whipping and blowing off walkways and driveways. After they were done on the grounds, they would set up various tents, awnings and white lights in the circle yard in front of the mansion. The forecast for the next day was sunny and hot, and they could use all the shade they could get.

For the moment, Joy was alone with her thoughts. A couple teenage girls from church had come to spend the day with Harper and Kinsley, and Chase had the boys busy helping outside, so Joy was free to let her mind wander while the vacuum hummed in her ears.

It had been over three weeks since Chase had taken Joy out to dance. Every day since then, they had found small pockets of time to spend alone together. At first, Joy thought it was by accident—but then she realized that both of them were seeking that time with each other. It might be cleaning up the kitchen for Mrs. Thompson, sitting on the pier to watch the sunset, taking a walk through downtown in the evening when all the stores were closed or just sitting in one of the parlors with a cup of coffee at the end of a long day. Joy had come to cherish those moments with Chase and looked forward to them every day.

It was during one of those evenings that Joy shared with Chase that the judge had legally revoked parental rights from the boys' mother. They were now orphans and she had started the official adoption process. Chase had let her talk out all her emotions that evening and offered her a shoulder to cry on as she mourned the boys' loss.

But today, there were no tears, only smiles as she ran the vacuum under one of the chairs in her bedroom. Though he never once pressured her, or pushed her to go faster than she was ready, she could no longer deny that she wanted a future with Chase Asher—had always wanted a future—and she was finally willing to admit the truth to herself.

A movement outside her bedroom window caught her eye and she paused to watch. Chase had all three boys at his side, each one wearing safety glasses. They stood in a line and walked around the circle drive with hand-held blowers. Kodi was so small, he struggled to hold his blower, but Chase was patient, because Kodi would hate to be left out.

Her heart warmed at the scene. It would be so much easier and faster to get the work done if the boys weren't under his feet, but Chase never once complained. On the contrary, he often called the boys to his side, knowing how much they loved to help.

She continued to vacuum, pondering all her feelings, until someone tapped her shoulder.

Joy jumped and turned—only to find Tom Winston standing behind her.

Turning off the machine, she placed her hand over her racing heart. "You scared me half to death!"

"Sorry about that." He was impeccably dressed in a dark gray suit, tie and shiny black shoes. "I only have a few minutes between appointments this morning and wanted to run something over to you."

He handed her a piece of paper. A picture of a large, charming farmhouse was in the upper-right-hand corner and beneath it were the details on the property. It was a five-bedroom house with three bathrooms, a new furnace and roof and ten acres of land.

But it was the price tag that caught her eye. Though it wasn't cheap, it was well within the range of possibility, especially with all the grants and donations she'd already received.

And she wouldn't need Chase to take out a mortgage for her.

"It just hit the market this morning," he said with a grin. "My buddy emailed it to me and said it'll go fast. I canceled several appointments this afternoon and scheduled a showing for us at four o'clock."

"This afternoon?"

"If we don't jump on it today, we'll lose it for sure. This house was recently renovated and the yard is immaculate. When I called the Realtor she said she already had two other showings scheduled this morning."

"I can't go this afternoon." Joy's shoulders slumped. "There are about fifteen people here today helping—I can't leave all of them to do my work."

"The farmhouse will go fas—"

"Joy?" Chase's voice called to her from the hall.

"I'm in the master bedroom," Joy answered.

Tom's jaw tightened and he shook his head. "Why does he always have to interrupt us?"

"We finished the mowing," Chase said, coming into the room, "do you want us to put up the ten—?" He paused when he saw Tom standing in her room.

Neither man spoke, so Joy stepped forward with the paper Tom had given her. "Tom stopped by to show me this property that just went up for sale. It's on the outskirts of town."

Chase frowned and took the sheet of paper. After a moment he said to Tom, "It was nice of you to come all the way over here to hand deliver it when you could have emailed the information." His voice dripped with sarcasm.

"I knew Joy wouldn't get a chance to check her email today." Tom stood with his arms crossed as he narrowed his eyes. "And I didn't want her to miss out on this property. If she likes it, she will need to make an offer by the end of today."

"Today?" Chase met Joy's gaze. "What about Bee Tree Hill?"

"Let's be real," Tom said in a no-nonsense tone. "Bee Tree Hill is a fantasy you've been dangling in front of Joy's nose to get what you want. As soon as she's hooked, you'll pull it out from under her. I'm just saving her the time and embarrassment and offering her something real and tangible."

Joy blinked several times at the unfair accusation. "Tom—"

"Why should Joy settle for second best when she has the opportunity to have something much better?" Chase asked.

"What you're offering is a pipe dream," Tom said. "There's nothing substantial and promising. You've allowed her to put her hopes and dreams into something that cannot possibly happen."

"We've put a lot of hard work into this dream," Chase countered. "It would be foolish to give up now."

"Stop," Joy said, as if she was interrupting an argument between the kids. "I think I'm old enough and smart enough to know what I want."

Each man offered something completely different. Tom represented stability and realism. He would only promise her what he had to give. He would offer no more and no less. Chase, on the other hand, represented adventure and romanticism. He promised that he would fight with her to reach for her dreams—even if it wasn't within his ability to give them to her. He would offer her as much as they could achieve together.

"Your volunteers will understand if you need to leave for an hour," Tom said impatiently. "I'm not asking you to come away with me for the entire day. But if you want to be guaranteed a home for you and the kids, you'll need to make this small sacrifice."

"We have hours of work ahead of us," Chase told her.

"If we don't get everything ready by tomorrow morning, we could miss the opportunity to make enough money to buy Bee Tree Hill."

Joy swallowed the uncertainty as she looked from one to the other.

"Think about the children," Tom said. "If you don't have a home for them next week, you might lose the boys."

On paper, the house that Tom presented to her was ideal. It was realistic and attainable, and as much as she loved Bee Tree Hill, and wanted to stay for the kids' sake, it wasn't as realistic and attainable.

"Don't give up on Bee Tree Hill," Chase pleaded. "This house was meant for you and the kids." The house was Chase's legacy—and now it was Harper and Kinsley's legacy, too. If she couldn't fight for that, what could she fight for?

"Joy?" Mrs. Thompson entered her bedroom with a rag in hand. "Oh, my," she said when she saw the men. "What's going on here?"

"I came to tell Joy about a house that went up for sale today." Tom took the sheet of paper from Chase and handed it to Mrs. Thompson. "I made an appointment to look at it at four. If she likes it, she'll need to make an offer right away. She can't hesitate."

Mrs. Thompson glanced at the paper. "I know this house. It's beautiful. You should go and look at it, Joy."

"What about all the volunteers? I can't leave them now."

"Oh, pish-posh," she said. "I was just coming up here to encourage you to get out of the house for a couple hours and take a deep breath. I have a shopping list that needs to be taken care of and I was going to send you to the store. We'll be working late tonight and getting up early tomorrow. We have everything under control here for now."

"You don't think—?"

"Go," Mrs. Thompson said, nodding. "Don't hesitate. Check out the house, pray about it and see if you have peace about making an offering."

Chase stood near Joy, watching her for her answer.

Joy took Mrs. Thompson's advice as often as possible and had never gone wrong. So then why did she feel like she was betraying Chase?

"I'll be back to pick you up in a couple hours," Tom said as he started to walk toward the door. "I've cleared the rest of my afternoon and evening, so I can run you to the grocery store when we're done looking at the farmhouse."

Joy found herself nodding, though she hadn't fully committed to going with him.

"See you soon," he said as he left the room.

"I think I just heard the timer for my cookies. I don't want them to burn." Mrs. Thompson scurried out of the room, leaving Joy alone with Chase.

Joy couldn't bring herself to look at him. "I know you're disappointed."

"Don't worry about me."

"What am I supposed to do?"

"Believe in your dreams."

"But what is there to believe in?" she whispered. "How can I be certain that we'll succeed?"

He gently tilted her face up to look at him. "You can't be certain that we'll succeed, Joy. None of us know what the future holds." His eyes were so clear, so full of hope and longing, pleasure swirled through her. "But you can be certain that I'm here to stay. Whether we succeed in buying Bee Tree Hill—or we end up buying a farmhouse—we will still have each other, and that's the most important thing we can be certain of."

She blinked several times, trying to comprehend what he'd just said. "Even if we don't buy Bee Tree Hill, you want to help me buy another home?"

"I want you and the kids to have a safe, loving home to live in. I hope it's Bee Tree Hill, but it doesn't have to be." He took a step closer to her and reached for her hand. "I've been trying to tell you—but I don't think you've been listening. I'm here to stay, Joy. I'm not going anywhere."

His hair was windblown and he smelled like fresh-cut grass, but he'd never looked better to her.

"If you'll let me," he said, "I'd like to stay in Timber Falls—no matter what happens with Bee Tree Hill."

It was almost exactly what he'd told her last time, the day before he left. *If you'll let me, I'd like to stay in Timber Falls until you graduate from college and then we can get married.*

She'd believed him last time—and she wanted to believe him this time, too. Over the past couple of months, he'd proved to her that he was there for good—that he wanted to make her happy. But she couldn't forget what Tom said. Was Chase using Bee Tree Hill to manipulate her feelings? She didn't want to believe it was true, but that didn't make it so.

"Let's get through the festival," she said. "And then we'll talk about the future." She grasped the vacuum again. "But I'm still going to take Mrs. Thompson's advice and look at the farmhouse."

Chase nodded. "If you think it's a good idea."

"I do."

He smiled, though there was sadness in his eyes. "I better get back outside and help set up the tents."

Joy watched him walk out of the room, her heart going with him. Just before he disappeared down the stairs, he winked, and she smiled.

The heat had been rising steadily throughout the day, and with it, the humidity. Chase wiped his forehead with the sleeve of his shirt and then took another stack of folding chairs off the back of the trailer they had borrowed from a neighbor. The church had graciously allowed them to borrow a hundred chairs and a dozen banquet tables, which Chase and the men were setting up under the half-dozen tents on the lawn.

"Should we start setting up chairs under the next tent?" Ryan asked Chase, wiping his forehead just like Chase had done.

"Why don't you and the boys grab some water bottles and a few cookies and take a break." Chase set down the stack of chairs. "You've been working hard."

Mrs. Thompson had brought fresh cookies and a cooler of water out to the men, but they hadn't taken a break yet.

Ryan nodded eagerly and then he ran to the refreshments with his brothers.

Chase grinned at Pastor Jacob, who was unloading another stack of chairs.

"You're a natural with those boys," Jacob said to Chase. "They have a lot of respect for you."

The unexpected compliment made Chase pause.

"Do you have younger siblings?" the pastor asked as he set the stack of chairs down.

"I'm an only child." Chase opened a folding chair and set it up next to the table.

"I would have never guessed." Jacob started to unfold

his chairs, too. "I've noticed a new light in Joy and the kids since you got here."

Chase stopped unfolding the chairs. How much did Pastor Jacob know about him and Joy? She wasn't the type of person to share her personal business with others—but maybe she had said something to her pastor. "They've been good for me, too."

Jacob smiled and nodded. "I've been praying for Joy for a long time now. You just might be the answer to those prayers."

Chase was the answer to a prayer? He had never thought of himself in that light—but now that he did, it gave him a sense of purpose he'd never felt before. "I don't know how much Joy has told you."

"She's told me a few things. I know Harper and Kinsley are yours."

"I left her four years ago because I was afraid to stand up against my father." It took Chase a second to compose his thoughts. "At the time, I didn't know about the girls."

"Ah." Jacob nodded. "I wondered."

"But now that I know, I don't want to mess things up again."

Jacob wiped his forehead and continued to nod. "When we make choices based on fear, we often make the wrong decision. It's the choices we make based on faith that really matter."

Chase considered his words and thought about the choices he had made. Each poor decision had been based in fear and had led to heartache and pain.

"But thank God that whatever the enemy intends for evil, God will use for good." Jacob took another stack of chairs off the trailer. "Nothing has been broken that can't be fixed, Chase. Jesus was a carpenter. He's in the business of mending and repairing."

Chase smiled. For years, he'd felt like a disappointment to his father and then to Joy. He'd made mistakes that felt impossible to fix—but maybe it wasn't up to him to do all the mending.

A car turned into the drive and Chase glanced up, hoping it was Joy. She had left two hours ago with Tom and he'd been counting down the minutes until they returned—but it wasn't Tom's car that pulled up the drive.

"Excuse me," Chase said to Jacob.

He walked toward the front door where the silver BMW came to a stop.

The driver's door and passenger door opened at the same time and Chase's pulse started to thrum.

Malcolm Asher stepped out of the BMW, a pair of dark sunglasses hiding his eyes. He stood tall and straight. His suit didn't have a wrinkle and every piece of his graying hair was in place. He glanced around the lawn, his lips turning down in disapproval.

"What's going on, Chase?" He closed the door and put his hands on his hips. "Why are all these people here and what are those tents doing on the lawn?"

Chase groaned. Why had his dad decided to show up now?

The other man stepped out of the passenger door, scanning the property. He also wore a suit, but he wasn't nearly as polished as Chase's father.

"Dad." Chase finally stopped in front of his father. "What are you doing here?"

Malcolm pulled his sunglasses off. "You've been wasting everyone's time, so I decided to come and take care of things myself." He pointed his glasses at Pastor Jacob and the boys. "What's the meaning of all this?"

It didn't pay to put off the inevitable. "We're having a festival here tomorrow."

"A festival?" Dad's lips curled in disgust. "Whatever for?"

"It's a—" Chase hesitated. His dad would never approve—but he couldn't hide the truth. "It's a fund-raiser for the family who is living here."

"A what?"

"A fund-raiser. The family who lives here needs housing, so the community is coming together to raise money for her and the kids." It was a true statement—though he'd chosen to leave out Joy's name—or the fact that she wanted to buy Bee Tree Hill.

One thing at a time.

"Don't you think you have better things to do with your time?" Dad shook his head, his blue eyes—so much like Chase's—full of disapproval.

"It's the least we could do for the family."

"We'll deal with this topic later." Malcolm turned away from Chase and nodded at his guest. "This is Conrad Tidwell. I believe you spoke."

Chase walked around the car and extended his hand to Tidwell. "I wasn't expecting you for two more days."

"Obviously." Dad opened the back door and pulled out a small suitcase. "We've been traveling all day. I'd like to freshen up before we give Conrad the tour. Show us to our rooms."

The house would be open for tours the next day, and all the rooms had been prepared for that purpose. If his dad and Mr. Tidwell took two of the rooms, it would disrupt the tours they had planned.

"I, ah—" Chase had no idea what to do with his father. "We're giving tours of the mansion tomorrow. I wasn't expecting you—there are no rooms available."

Malcolm's jaw clenched and the muscles in his cheek rippled. "I have no time for this nonsense, Chase." He placed his thumb and forefinger on the bridge of his nose and closed his eyes briefly. "You need to call off this festival immediately. We have business to take care of."

"We can't call off the festival." Chase looked between Tidwell and his father, anger filling his chest. "Countless people have worked tirelessly for this event. There's no way we can cancel now."

His father didn't like when Chase contradicted him— and he saw it in the way his eyes snapped—but Chase didn't care. Joy was depending on this festival and he would not let Malcolm Asher change her plans.

"What would people think if you canceled it now?" Chase asked.

It was his father's only insecurity, and Chase knew when to play that card.

"Fine," Malcolm said with his teeth clenched. "But Mr. Tidwell and I will need rooms—and I don't care how it affects everyone's plans."

"There are rooms in the carriage house." Chase pointed down the hill. "It's the best I can offer right now."

Malcolm opened the back door and tossed his suitcase back inside. He slammed the door. "Fine."

His father got into the driver's seat and Conrad quietly got into the passenger side.

"I'll meet you at the carriage house," Chase told his father.

It would take his father a couple minutes to drive around the back of the mansion and reach the carriage house, so Chase jogged over to Jacob. "Something has come up. Can you keep an eye on the boys?"

"Of course."

Though the pastor didn't ask for information, Chase felt the need to explain. "That was my father. He flew in from Seattle. I wasn't expecting him."

"I gathered that much." Jacob gave him an encouraging smile. "The boys and I will be fine."

"Thanks." Chase turned away, but then he looked back at Jacob. "If Joy returns—can you let me tell her about my dad?" The last thing he wanted was Joy to hear that his father was here from someone else.

"Absolutely."

Chase waved at the boys as he passed them. "I'll be back in a little while. Pastor Jacob will keep an eye on you."

Ryan gave Chase the thumbs-up and grinned.

Chase returned his smile, though he didn't feel like smiling.

He jogged down the hill to reach the carriage house just as his father pulled up.

Everything within Chase wanted to revolt against this intrusion—but he knew the only way to deal with his father was to face him head-on. Come what may.

Chapter Fourteen

Chase had quickly washed his hands and face and changed into clean clothes, but now he paced at the bottom of the steps outside the carriage house waiting for his father and Mr. Tidwell. Thankfully, Mrs. Thompson had fresh bedding in each of the rooms, even though they hadn't been used in years. She was always prepared for everything and Chase was never more appreciative of her forethought than today.

Mr. Tidwell opened the carriage-house door and walked down the steps. He looked around the property as he descended the stairs. "It's nice to finally meet you in person," he said to Chase with a smile. The man was about as old as Malcolm, but he wasn't as severe or cold. He was a short man with a head full of dark curly hair, deep wrinkles on his tanned face and small eyes, which didn't miss much.

"It's a pleasure to meet you, too," Chase said, though it couldn't be further from the truth.

"I haven't seen much of the property, but what I have seen, I like." Tidwell grinned. "I can't wait to see the rest."

"There's no other property like Bee Tree Hill."

"I've been looking for a place like this for years."

"Do you plan to relocate to Minnesota?"

"No." Tidwell spread his feet and crossed his arms. "I'm in the hospitality business and I've been interested in building a resort on the Upper Mississippi for years." He moved with nervous energy. "I have a ski resort in Vermont, a spa in Northern California, a large bed-and-breakfast in Savannah and a hotel in Denver. I've been looking for just the right spot in Minnesota, and I think I might have found it."

Chase frowned. "Are you looking at creating another bed-and-breakfast with the mansion?"

Tidwell shook his head. "No. It's the land and access to the river that interests me. I want to build a resort and marina, so I'll tear down all the buildings and start from scratch."

Chase's mouth slipped open. "Tear down the buildings?"

Tidwell squinted and looked at the carriage house and then up to the mansion. "I'm afraid it would all have to go. I have no need for the houses."

"What?" Chase couldn't believe his ears. "The mansion is irreplaceable. It was built by my great-grandfather in 1898. It's the very heart of this community. If it weren't for the Asher family, Timber Falls wouldn't—"

"Chase." Malcolm Asher appeared behind Chase, a frown on his face. "That's enough."

"We can't let someone tear down Bee Tree Hill."

"It's no concern of ours what Conrad chooses to do with the property."

"It concerns us a great deal." Chase could hardly believe what his father was saying. "The Asher Corporation would be nothing without Bee Tree Hill."

Malcolm shrugged as if it didn't matter. "It no longer serves a purpose."

"It's a home—a legacy."

"We'll talk about this later." Malcolm moved around Chase to join Tidwell.

"We'll talk about this now." Chase had never spoken to his father this way, but maybe it was time to start. Bee Tree Hill didn't belong just to his father—it belonged to all the Ashers—including Harper and Kinsley.

"Dad, I need to speak to you. Alone."

"Now isn't the time—"

"Mr. Tidwell, could you please excuse us?" Chase wouldn't let this wait. Now that his father was here, it was time to share the truth about a few things.

"Of course. I'll walk down to the river and take a look for myself." Tidwell scurried off without another word.

Malcolm turned to Chase, his face red and his nostrils flaring. "Chase, you are out of line."

"How could you sell Bee Tree Hill? I just told Tidwell this place is the heart of Timber Falls, but it's also the heart of the Asher family."

"It's just a place—and it's worth a lot of money."

"Is everything about money to you?" Chase hated that his father's very existence revolved around the pursuit of wealth. Malcolm had sacrificed everything for his money—and for what? He had no healthy relationships, his family despised him, his wife had left him and everyone who worked for him was afraid of him.

"What else is there?" Malcolm asked.

"Family, love—faith."

"Hogwash." Malcolm turned to look for Tidwell. "We need to catch up to—"

"I want to keep Bee Tree Hill."

"No." Malcolm rubbed the bridge of his nose again. "We've been over this."

"It should stay in the Asher family."

"You're no better than your aunt Constance. She's so focused on the past, she can't see the future."

Aunt Constance was the reason Chase had chosen to come to Bee Tree Hill over four years ago to begin with. It was her influence, and love of their family, that had piqued Chase's interest in their Minnesota home. "Aunt Constance once told me that we'll lose sight of where we're going if we forget where we have been." Chase hadn't thought about his aunt in a long time—too long. "She would be horrified if she knew you planned to sell Bee Tree Hill to a man who wants to tear it down."

"It's a good thing she's not in charge, then."

An idea started to form and Chase had to look away from his father to let it develop completely. Aunt Constance might not be the president and CEO of the Asher Corporation, but she, along with several other family members, were stockholders in the company. If enough of them sided with Chase, could they persuade the board of directors to veto Malcolm's decision to sell the property?

"Why would you want this place?" Malcolm finally asked, his disdain for the property evident in the scowl on his face. "Your life is in Seattle. This place is nothing but a money pit."

Chase let his eyes wander around the property. The fort stood at the bottom of the hill and had already provided the boys with countless hours of fun. The chickens near the barn had produced dozens of eggs and been a place for Chase and Joy to teach the kids lessons about responsibility. The pier near the water had become a respite for Chase and Joy to unwind at the end of the day and spend time getting to know one another again.

Everywhere he looked, he saw what mattered most.

"My life is here now." He thought about his daughters in the mansion. "I want to pass on Bee Tree Hill to my children."

"You lost your chance to become a father when Tamara left you."

"No." Chase shook his head, ready to tell his father the truth. "I'm already a father."

Malcolm stared at Chase, his eyes narrowing. "What did you say?"

"When I returned to Bee Tree Hill, it was Joy Gordon who was still living here." He straightened his back. "You remember Joy, the young woman I was in love with when you came to take me away from here."

His father crossed his arms, but didn't say a word.

"It turns out she was pregnant with twins—my daughters—when I left. Uncle Morgan invited her to stay here, because he felt responsible to care for his family—your family."

"How can you be so foolish, Chase?"

"The only foolish thing I did was leave here four years ago."

"I remember that girl well. She was trying to get a free ride and she found it. Those kids probably aren't even yours, but she knew Morgan would feel responsible—"

"They are mine." Chase clenched his fists. "You don't even know Joy—"

"I know her kind. They're all the same. We have money and they want it."

"You're wrong about her."

"Is she the one pressuring you to keep Bee Tree Hill?"

"Of course not."

"I suppose she doesn't need to pressure you. It's apparent that she has other means of controlling you."

Chase had no time to argue with his father. And the longer he stood near him, the angrier he became. "I have things to do."

"Don't walk away from me," his father demanded.

But Chase was done bending to the will of Malcolm Asher. He was a grown man and he was going to take his future—and the future of his family—into his own hands.

As he walked away from his father, he took his phone out of his pocket and looked for his aunt's number. He had a call to make and he couldn't do it fast enough.

"Mama!"

Joy set the groceries on the counter in the kitchen, surprised to find the room empty, and turned to meet Ryan as he walked into the room. "Where have you been?" she asked with a smile.

Tom was bringing in the other groceries, but he hadn't made it inside yet.

"Chase's dad is here," Ryan said breathlessly. "He's going to sell Bee Tree Hill to someone who wants to tear it all down."

"What?" Joy took the sugar out of a bag, uncertain she'd heard him correctly. "Who's here?"

"Chase's dad."

The world seemed to come to a halt as Joy anchored her hands on the counter for support. "His dad is here?"

"I was hiding near the carriage house." Ryan's cheeks were bright red. "Chase's dad is going to sell Bee Tree Hill and the short man is going to tear it all down. And Chase said he's a dad and he was angry at his dad and his dad was angry—"

"Whoa, whoa." Joy put up her hand to stop him from rambling. "Where's Chase?"

"He's on his phone behind the house."

Tom entered the kitchen at that moment, his arms full of grocery bags. "Where do you want them?"

"Here." Joy motioned absentmindedly to the counter. "Will you excuse me for a minute?"

"Sure."

"Are you going to talk to Chase?" Ryan asked. "Don't let the man tear down the house."

Tom frowned. "What's he talking about?"

"I don't know." Joy walked to the door. "I need to find Chase."

She pushed open the back door and walked down the stairs, feeling like she was blind. She stumbled and caught herself, her heart racing.

An expensive, unfamiliar car sat parked in front of the carriage house. Joy's throat became dry and she started to pray. Was Mr. Asher at Bee Tree Hill again? The last time he'd been there, he'd torn her whole life apart.

She rounded the corner and found Chase pacing behind the mansion, his phone to his ear, his free hand gesturing all around him. He nodded as he spoke—and then he pulled the phone away and tapped the screen.

"Chase?" Joy jogged the last few yards.

He turned and the look on his face told her all she needed to know.

"He's here?" she asked, choking on the words.

"I had no idea he was coming, Joy. He showed up unexpectedly."

"Why is he here?"

"He brought Mr. Tidwell—even though I wasn't expecting him until Sunday. I didn't know he'd be coming with my father."

"Mr. Tidwell?" Joy shook her head. "Who is he?"

Chase ran his hand through his hair and rested it on his neck. "He's an investor."

"You had an investor coming on Sunday and you didn't tell me?"

"I didn't want to worry you."

"Worry me?"

"You have enough going on as it is."

"How long have you known about Mr. Tidwell?"

Chase didn't respond immediately, making Joy's heart pound even harder.

"I've known almost since the beginning."

"You've had an investor lined up since the beginning— and you didn't bother to tell me?"

"What did it matter?"

"What did it matter?" Joy stared at him with incredulity. "It mattered a great deal. All this time, I've been working for nothing."

"It's not nothing." Chase frowned. "If it wasn't Tidwell, it would have been someone else."

"What other things have you kept from me, Chase?"

He shook his head. "I haven't kept anything from you."

"Anything, except an appointment with an investor." She couldn't believe he'd kept this information to himself. Was Tom right? Had Chase been using Bee Tree Hill to manipulate her? Did he have plans to sell it all along?

"Let's try to focus on the festival," Chase said. "Take one thing at a time. I have a call in to my aunt to—"

"I need to go." She couldn't think straight with Chase in front of her. "I have things to do. Tom needs to call the Realtor about the farmhouse."

She started to turn away, but Chase stopped her. "What about the farmhouse?"

"I—I decided to make an offer." At that very moment. When she had looked at the farmhouse, it had been nice, but it didn't feel like home. She had decided to let the opportunity pass and trust that God had a better plan for her—but now? Now she didn't have any other options. Chase's dad was at Bee Tree Hill with an interested investor. If she let the farmhouse go, she and the children might be living in a two-bedroom apartment at the end of the week.

"You're going to make an offer on the farmhouse?" Chase shook his head. "Why?"

"Because I need a home for my children," she said, louder than she intended. She couldn't hide her anger or disappointment in him. Why hadn't he been honest with her about the investor? "They need stability and security."

"Don't make a rash decision." He took her hands in his. "Let's see how the festival goes and then—"

"It will be too late." She pulled her hands away. When he touched her, she couldn't think straight—she needed to get away from him to clear her head. She turned again and walked toward the house.

She had been silly to believe that she could keep Bee Tree Hill.

Had she been silly to believe she could trust Chase, too? Had he told his dad about the girls?

Suddenly, nothing else mattered. She needed to find her daughters.

Joy began to run and didn't stop until she reached the girls' bedroom.

Chapter Fifteen

Evening sunshine slanted across the girls' bedroom floor as Joy pushed open the door and found Harper and Kinsley playing on the carpet with the teenagers who had come by that day to babysit them.

"Mama!" Kinsley said. She held up a tower she'd made out of pink-and-purple blocks. "You like?"

Joy put her hand over her heart and leaned against the doorframe. The girls were safe.

Harper ran across the floor and put her hands up to Joy. "Hold you," she said.

Picking up her daughter, Joy pulled her into a tight hug and smiled at the teenagers babysitting. "Mrs. Thompson is serving supper under one of the tents in the front yard. Why don't you two go on out to eat. I'll bring the girls in a bit."

The young ladies smiled shyly and left the room.

Joy sat on the bed and motioned Kinsley to come to her.

She held her girls on her lap, praying Mr. Asher would leave Bee Tree Hill and never come back. No one frightened Joy like he did. He was rich, powerful and merciless. He had hurt her once and he had the ability to hurt her even more this time.

"I hungry," Kinsley said to Joy.

"You're always hungry," she said with a smile.

Kinsley climbed off Joy's lap and tugged her hand. "Let's eat."

She couldn't keep the girls locked away in their room forever—but she didn't want to bring them out onto the lawn where Mr. Asher could easily see them.

Instead, she took the back stairs down to the kitchen and set the girls at the table.

Everyone was still outside, which she was thankful for. She didn't have the heart to see anyone right now.

She took a couple graham crackers from the pantry to tide the girls over until she could get them something a little more substantial. As they crunched away, she poured them some milk and cut up some grapes, which she put onto their plates.

Her hands shook as she worked, but it felt good to have something to keep her busy. There was still so much to do for the festival, but all she could focus on was keeping the girls close by her side.

After they were settled with their grapes, she pulled out some leftover beef-and-vegetable stew and started to warm it up on the stovetop.

The back door creaked open and Joy looked up from the stove.

Malcolm Asher stood on the back porch looking into the kitchen through the open door.

The spoon in Joy's hand clattered to the floor and she took a protective step toward the girls.

Mr. Asher walked into the kitchen without an invitation, his shiny black shoes tapping against the wood floor. His blue eyes were cold and calculating as he took in Joy and the girls in one slow, steady sweep of the room.

Everything in her wanted to grab the girls and run, but she froze, her heart pounding, her hands sweating and her legs trembling.

Memories from their last encounter crowded her mind, making her feel dirty, tarnished and unworthy.

"Hello," Kinsley said to Malcolm as she picked up half a grape. "You like grapes?"

"Are these the children?" Mr. Asher asked Joy, his voice devoid of emotion. "The illegitimate twins you claim belong to Chase?"

Joy's chest rose and fell with deep, unsteady breaths. All her life, she'd been told she was unwanted—but that was her story, not her children's.

"No." She knew what illegitimate meant, but it did not describe her daughters. "These are Chase's legitimate daughters."

"You know what I meant."

"Yes." Somehow, somewhere deep inside where her love and devotion sprang forth for her daughters, she was able to muster up the courage to speak back to Mr. Asher. "And you know what I meant, too."

He was an impressive man—handsome, tall, strong, and well dressed. If she passed him on the street, she'd give him a wide berth. Here, in the kitchen, he dominated the space.

"I thought I made myself clear where you're concerned." Mr. Asher spoke down to her, like she was a dirty servant. "You were able to deceive my uncle, but I am not as gullible as the old man. I know what you're after and you will not receive it from me or my son."

"I'm not after anything." The stew hissed and bubbled on the stove behind her, but Joy ignored it.

"If you want money, you won't get any," he said.

"I don't want your money."

Mr. Asher turned his attention on the girls and studied them closely.

Joy took another step toward them and put her hands on Kinsley's shoulders, her pulse picking up speed.

"If it's money you want," Malcolm adjusted his cuffs, "I will agree to a paternity test—but if it comes back positive, I will prove you're incompetent and ensure that the girls are removed from your influence."

Joy's mouth fell open as she stared at the man.

"Is that what you want, Miss Gordon?" His lips grew thin. "Or would you like to slip away quietly and never bother my family again?"

"You not nice," Kinsley said to Mr. Asher with a frown.

Harper climbed out of her booster and ran around the table to stand behind Joy.

Joy knew what it felt like to be raised without a father, and she did not wish that upon her girls—but she couldn't lose them, either. "I don't want anything from you or Chase," she whispered.

"Then leave him alone." Malcolm's voice held no room for debate. "He made his choice to leave four years ago and he'll make it again. I know my son."

Joy's chest tightened and tears gathered in her eyes, but she would not allow herself to cry in front of this man. He'd only scoff at her.

She lifted Kinsley out of her booster and picked up Harper. It wasn't easy to hold both girls, but she needed them close. "I will be out of the house in three days."

"Good." He let his eyes roam over her and the girls. "I never want to hear from you again. Do you understand?"

Without giving him the benefit of an answer, she

turned and left the kitchen through another door leading into the foyer. If she wasn't committed to the festival and all the trouble her friends, neighbors and community members had gone to, she would have left that night. But she owed everyone a festival—and she would do her best to make sure it was the best festival it could be.

But as soon as it was over, she and the kids would leave Bee Tree Hill and the Asher family for good.

Chase entered the house through the front door, Ryan, Jordan and Kodi at his side. When he saw her, his face filled with concern.

"What happened?" he asked.

She shook her head, afraid she'd start to cry if she tried to answer him.

"Ryan," Chase said, "can you please take everyone out to Mrs. Thompson?"

"No." Joy would not let the girls out of her sight. "I will take them to her."

She tried to move past Chase, but he put his hand on her arm. "I'm sorry, Joy. I didn't mean to keep Mr. Tidwell from you. I was going to tell you after the festival—I just didn't want to bother you with one more thing to worry about right now."

It wasn't about Mr. Tidwell or Bee Tree Hill anymore. It was about Malcolm Asher and her daughters. She couldn't risk his ire. If she made him angry, he'd try to hurt her with the one thing that could destroy her.

Losing her children.

"Don't worry about it," she said to Chase, trying to control her features so the children wouldn't be concerned. She motioned for the boys to go out the front door. "We have a lot more to do before tomorrow," she told them. "Let's get busy."

She started to leave the foyer, but Chase held out his hands. "Do you want me to take one of the girls for you?"

Joy held them tighter and shook her head. "We're fine."

She wasn't fine—but she wouldn't ask Chase for any more help.

The door closed behind Joy, and Chase let out a weary sigh. He had broken her trust again and he didn't know how to repair it. She was hurt and angry, and rightfully so. He should have told her about Tidwell—but it was too late.

The smell of burnt food wafted from the kitchen. Chase pushed open the door and found the pot on the stove. He frowned. Hadn't Joy just come from here? Why would she leave food on the stove to burn?

He crossed the room and turned off the burner.

A movement outside the porch window caught his eyes. He went to the window and saw the back of his dad's head as he walked down the hill toward the carriage house—his hands in his pockets, his gait even and steady—and then Chase knew. His father had said something to Joy and that's why she had just walked out upset.

Dread mounted in Chase's heart and he pushed open the door. He couldn't let his father destroy everything he and Joy had built these past two months.

"Dad," Chase called to his father.

Malcolm turned at the sound of Chase's voice. His eyes narrowed as he watched Chase approach.

The heat and humidity had caused Chase to start sweating again—yet his father looked as cool and composed as he would in any situation.

"What did you say to Joy?" Chase demanded when he finally came to stand before his father.

"I simply told her what you have failed to say. I want her gone. She agreed to leave in seventy-two hours. You're done with her and those children for good."

Chase shook his head. "I won't let her leave."

"You have no choice."

Maybe Chase believed that in the past, but he knew better now. "I always have a choice."

His father stared at him for a few moments. "I've struggled to make you understand what's expected of you."

"I know what you expect."

"No." Malcolm shook his head, his voice rising. "You have no idea what type of sacrifices I've made to be where I'm at today. I expect the same from you—yet you constantly disappoint me."

There was no wind, just hot, thick air. Chase tried to take a deep breath, but he struggled. He had been a disappointment to his father his whole life, but suddenly he realized that the trouble wasn't with him—it was with his father. No one could ever please Malcolm Asher—no matter how much they tried. "I know exactly what you sacrificed for your work and I'm not willing to make the same mistake."

"Mistake?" Malcolm lifted his eyebrows. "Is running a multimillion-dollar company a mistake?"

"No." Chase shook his head. "But sacrificing a relationship with your son and pushing away everyone who ever loved you is a mistake." He was sick to his stomach thinking about all the wasted years he and Joy could have had together. "But the biggest mistake of all is the one you're making right now."

"And what's that?"

"Threatening the future relationship with your granddaughters."

Chapter Sixteen

Despite the heartache and the uncertainty, Joy stood with a smile on her face late the next afternoon as Bee Tree Hill hummed with activity. Hundreds of people had come to the estate to support Joy and the children and to celebrate the legacy of the Asher family in Timber Falls.

As the sun made its descent in the western sky, all around her familiar faces glowed with excitement as people took house tours, sampled Mrs. Thompson's caramel corn, apple pie, ice cream and freshly squeezed lemonade, played carnival games, took rides in vintage automobiles and visited with friends and neighbors. Her own children took great pride in sharing their home with the community and, even if it was just for one more day, she thanked God that they had a home to be proud of.

Ryan, Jordan and Kodi played with their friends, while Kinsley and Harper were in the care of the teenage girls who had babysat them yesterday. Joy had kept them within her line of sight all day, though she had been too busy to play the games or sample the treats with them.

Chase was busy helping with the silent auction, hauling supplies for Mrs. Thompson and greeting people who had come just to meet him. She had done a good job

"They're not my gr—"

"They are—and they will continue to be yours for as long as you live."

His father inhaled a deep breath through his nose, his chest rising and then falling in a steady stream of air. "I've warned you before, Chase. If you want to inherit the Asher Corporation, and everything I've worked for— you will walk away from that woman today. If you don't, you and I are finished."

It was the same ultimatum his father had given him last time, but this time, Chase knew what was more important. This time, he was a father and even though he'd only known for a few weeks, he was willing to do whatever it would take to protect his daughters.

He'd learned the hard way what life looked like without Joy.

Instead of fear his father, Chase felt sorry for him. "You'd sacrifice a relationship with your only child and grandchildren?"

Malcolm Asher's shoulders fell ever so slightly—but then he lifted them again and said, "I'll do whatever I need for the company."

"And I'll do whatever I need for the family."

"I am your family."

"You're right—but so are those girls. And the best thing I can do for them is love them unconditionally and stand up to their grandfather."

His father stared at him for a long time. "You'd give up your inheritance for a woman and two little girls?"

Chase shook his head. "No. I'm embracing my inheritance—a legacy of dedication, commitment and selflessness, which Uncle Morgan taught me and showed to Joy when I was not here to do it myself."

The look of contempt slipped away from his father's

face and he appeared truly baffled. "You don't care about the Asher Corporation?"

"I care very much—but if I have to choose, I choose family over business—and I have a feeling most Ashers would, too."

The first hint of cool air blew across the Mississippi and ruffled the leaves on the trees along the riverbank. A blue heron flew low across the water and a swarm of bugs danced over the surface.

Chase faced his father, ready to do what he should have done all along. He would stand up for himself and those he loved.

"Where does this leave us?" Malcolm asked.

"I hope it leaves us as family." Chase realized he was standing exactly like his father, his shoulders high, his back straight, his arms crossed. "I plan to stay in Timber Falls and make a home for my family."

The muscles in Malcolm's cheek flexed and he studied Chase. "If you stay, you'll have to do it on your own. You will be out of a job and out of my will. I will not give you Bee Tree Hill—or anything else you think you're entitled to."

Chase had expected nothing more from his father. He wanted to pretend he wasn't disappointed, but he was. "If that's how you feel—"

"I expect you to leave within seventy-two hours, as well." His father lifted his chin. "As far as I'm concerned, you are no longer a part of the Asher Corporation. Your job is terminated, effective immediately."

Chase nodded. "And the festival?"

His father waved aside the question. "How can I stop it now without looking like an ogre? Have your festival— but I want everyone gone in three days. No exceptions.

If anyone remains, I will have them forcib from the premises."

A heaviness overwhelmed Chase as he fa ther for the last time. "My door will always t you, if you change your mind."

Malcolm harrumphed and turned around walking toward the carriage house. No doubt Mr. Tidwell a tour of the property and conduct I ness as if nothing had happened—but even if he w acknowledge the loss, Chase would.

avoiding him since yesterday, which hadn't been hard to do with all the preparation that had kept her busy into the wee hours of the morning.

His father and the investor were still on the property, but had avoided making an appearance. No one mentioned Malcolm Asher's presence and Joy was thankful for that. The less she had to interact with him, the better.

"Tabitha!" Joy caught sight of her friend from church and opened her arms for a hug. "I didn't expect to see you here today."

Tabby Rutten pushed a long stroller containing her fifteen-month-old triplets. The little boys were dressed in identical blue jean shorts and blue-and-white-striped shirts. They wore wide-brimmed hats and watched the excitement of the festival with big blue eyes.

"We wouldn't miss this for the world," Tabby said as she hugged Joy. "Adam's around here somewhere." She shaded her eyes to look for her husband. "He's more social than I am."

The boys were a handful and Tabby liked to stay close to home with them. She attended church, but rarely took the boys out to social events. Joy was honored that she'd come to her fund-raiser.

Pastor Jacob and his daughter Maggie walked toward Joy. Maggie held a candied apple in one hand and a bag of cotton candy in the other. Jacob held her balloons and the doll she'd won at the fishing-pond game.

"Tabby," Pastor Jacob said, "it's good to see you."

Maggie left her father's side and knelt near the boys. She grinned, her mouth a sticky mess. "Hi," she said to the babies.

One of them reached for Maggie's candied apple, but she pulled it away and said, "No, no, little boy."

The baby started to cry and Maggie's little mouth turned down, as if she might cry, too.

Tabby leaned over to pick him up. "Shh, Carter." She bounced him and winked at Maggie. "It's okay, sweetheart."

"Mags, why don't you step away from the babies so they're not tempted by your sweets?" Pastor Jacob said.

Maggie did as she was told. When she was far enough away, her smile returned and she said, "Daddy, can I have a brother?"

Joy didn't miss the sadness in Jacob's eyes, but he smiled for his daughter's sake. "I think I have my hands full with just one of you."

"You can come over any time you want," Tabby said to Maggie, "and play with the boys."

"May I, Daddy?" Maggie asked, jumping up and down, her eyes shining with excitement.

"That sounds like a great idea," Jacob said. "As long as you're helpful and not more trouble for Mrs. Rutten."

"I'm sure she'll be a lot of help." Tabby set Carter on her hip and looked over the upper grounds of Bee Tree Hill. "You've had a wonderful turnout, Joy."

"We have." Joy nodded, trying to savor the moment. "I had no idea so many people would come."

"You're a blessed woman," Pastor Jacob said with a genuine smile. "Wealthy beyond compare with friends who love you and your family."

It was true. Even if she couldn't make enough money to save Bee Tree Hill, she was wealthy in the ways that mattered most.

The alarm on Joy's phone rang and she pulled it out of her pocket to turn it off. "If you'll excuse me, I need to go close the silent auction."

She left Tabby, Pastor Jacob and the kids and walked

to the tents set up on the north side of the lawn. Under the tents, a dozen tables were laden with the silent auction donations she'd collected.

Chase was already there, pulling the auction sheets. A handful of people lingered to see if they won, and then walked away, leaving Chase and Joy alone.

He stopped at one donation sheet and shook his head, a smile on his face.

Joy started to work from the opposite end and pulled the papers—but then he noticed her and he held up the sheet he'd been smiling at.

It was the bachelor auction, which Marcy Hanover had suggested—and won.

"She bid an alarming amount of money," Chase said.

On the opposite side of the lawn, a small band began to play and the lights strung in the trees turned on. A dance was scheduled for the evening, and already children and a few older couples stepped onto the dance floor.

A quick perusal of the other auction items showed Joy that everyone had bid high today. Warmth filled her chest as she finished pulling the papers.

Chase reached her side and handed all the other sheets to her.

"Thank you," she said.

He stood close to her. "I haven't had a chance to talk to you since yesterday."

"We've both been busy." She focused on organizing the papers. The church secretary sat at a table near the entrance to Bee Tree Hill. She'd been there most of the day, selling tickets and overseeing all the money transactions. She had also volunteered to take the auction payments, so Joy needed to get the papers to her as soon as possible.

"Did you make an offer on the farmhouse?" he asked.

Joy finally looked at him. "Yes, last night."

He studied her, his eyes so blue and tender. "Was it accepted?"

She swallowed and shuffled the papers again. "I don't know. I haven't heard from Tom today." She started to leave the tent. "I need to get these to Mrs. Anderson."

"Joy." Chase stepped in front of her. "I'm sorry about my father—I know he said things yesterday—"

"It's fine—"

"It's not fine. I don't know what he said, but I can imagine—"

"Don't worry about it." She continued to move toward Mrs. Anderson. "The children and I will be gone the day after tomorrow."

"I'll be gone then, too."

Joy pulled the papers close to her chest, and tried not to react to his statement. She knew he would eventually return to Seattle—so then why was she so disappointed?

"I spoke to my father," he said as he tried to keep up with her. "He gave me an—"

"Chase!" Marcy Hanover waved at him, her voice high with excitement. She intercepted Chase, three of her friends hovering around her. "I won the auction, didn't I?"

Chase had no choice but to stop. "I believe you did."

"Wonderful." Marcy wrapped her arm through his. "I wanted to chat about our date."

Joy continued to walk away from him. Whatever he had to say, she didn't want to hear. She didn't want to know what his father had offered him. A raise? A promotion?

The music swirled around her as she handed the papers to Mrs. Anderson.

When she turned back to the survey the scene, she found more of Marcy's friends surrounding Chase.

He looked her way, but she refused to meet his gaze.

Instead, she looked for the girls. They were not by the games, or near the refreshment tables, and they were not on the dance floor.

Her heart started to pound and she rushed toward the house. Maybe they had gone inside for some reason.

She moved along the edge of the festival and entered the house, forcing herself to smile at a group of people as they finished their tour.

Kinsley's giggle met Joy's ears before she saw her daughters in the front parlor with the teenagers who were watching them.

Joy's pulse evened out and she took a deep, steadying breath.

"We'll be starting the last tour of the day in five minutes," one of the volunteers said in the foyer to a group who had just entered.

The festival was almost over.

All that was left was the dance, which would end in a few hours.

She had been so focused on the festival the past two days, she hadn't seriously given thought to how she would pack and move in forty-eight hours. Where would they go until she could purchase a home? She didn't own any furniture, because she'd never lived on her own, but that presented more difficulties to overcome. Not only would she have to find a home, but she'd also have to furnish it, as well.

A headache began to form and she stopped to take several deep breaths.

She needed to focus on getting through the festival and then worry about the rest tomorrow.

The evening was now upon them and the upper lawn of Bee Tree Hill was lit by hundreds of white lights hanging from the trees. Chase stood on the outskirts of the crowd watching as people danced, laughed and visited under the charming lights. A gentle breeze drifted over the lawn, making the branches sway to the rhythm of the music.

He searched the faces to find Joy, but she was not among them. It had been almost an hour since he'd seen her last when he had been intercepted by Marcy and her entourage. He had wanted to tell Joy about the conversation he'd had with his father, but decided it was probably best that they'd been interrupted. The conversation could wait for a more private moment when everyone was gone.

The band played "Wonderful Tonight," and Chase wished he could find Joy and ask her to dance. He still remembered what it felt like to dance with her the last time.

The phone in his back pocket began to vibrate and he pulled it out. Aunt Constance. This was the call he'd been thinking about all day.

Stepping away from the noise of the dance, Chase walked around the back side of the house and answered the phone. "Hello."

"Chase?" Aunt Constance was the oldest female relative of the Asher family, but she was by far the most important.

"Hello, Aunt Constance."

"How are you, dear?" Her voice had aged along with her, though Chase knew she was still an active lady.

"The festival I told you about has been an amazing success." He wanted to talk to her about the other family members and what they wanted to do with Bee Tree Hill, but he knew she would be interested in hearing about the festival.

"I knew the citizens would come out to support Bee Tree Hill. I still think of Timber Falls as home, even though I haven't lived there for over eighty years now. They are some of the very best people."

"I couldn't agree more. I only wish I had grown up here."

"Sometimes you can't choose how you begin, but you can choose how you end."

That was a truth Chase had come to embrace.

"Which brings me to the reason for this call," Aunt Constance said with a bit of excitement in her voice. "It's taken me all day yesterday and today to call the rest of the family, but we've come to a very important decision."

The sounds of the festival faded away as Chase looked out over the lower lawn of Bee Tree Hill estate. It was dark, but fireflies floated on the breeze, offering flashes of light among the trees.

"We all agree that Bee Tree Hill should be preserved and the history saved from an investor."

Chase's pulse picked up speed. Alone, he could do nothing to stop his father, but with the backing of the rest of his family, Malcolm Asher would not have enough power to stand against them.

"Everyone I spoke to has pledged a substantial amount of money to put into a trust," Aunt Constance continued. "We want to maintain the property and save it for future generations of Asher family members."

"I'm speechless," Chase said, shaking his head.

"I personally called each board member of the Asher Corporation and told them our wishes, and they all agreed that they would not authorize your father to sell the property unless they had our consent."

Chase could hardly believe what he was hearing. All along, he and Joy had tried to save the property on their own, when all he needed was the support of his family to make it happen.

"As part of the trust, we will take control of the property away from the corporation and put it into the hands of a board of trustees chosen from among our family." He could hear a smile in her voice. "And when I told everyone about Miss Gordon and the work she's done in the community, we all agreed that Bee Tree Hill should continue to be a place of refuge for children in need. Morgan was the first to open his door to help them, through Miss Gordon, and we want to honor that gesture by continuing that legacy. We plan to start a nonprofit organization for that purpose."

Chase couldn't stop grinning.

"The Bible tells us that true religion is helping widows and orphans in their need," Aunt Constance said, "and that's what we want to do through Bee Tree Hill. What do you think of that?"

"I couldn't be more thrilled."

"Good." She sounded pleased. "Because we would like to offer you the job as the executive director of the estate and organization, with an annual income that will match the one you're currently receiving from the Asher Corporation. If you accept, we can work out the details later. The family hopes to meet at the estate within the next month to have our first annual reunion and the first meeting for the Bee Tree Hill Trust and organization."

It wouldn't take Chase another moment to consider her offer. "I will gladly become the executive director."

"Wonderful! That's what we were all hoping to hear."

"And I will have everything ready for the family reunion next month." He hadn't seen his extended family since a funeral several years ago. "I am already looking forward to seeing everyone again."

"And we're all looking forward to being at Bee Tree Hill with you. I can't tell you how happy it makes me to know that the Asher family will continue to live on the property and perpetuate the legacy our parents started there over a hundred and twenty years ago."

"I hope I make everyone proud."

"You already have, Chase." She paused and then said, "Would you like me to tell your father our plans?"

Chase glanced toward the carriage house. The lights were on inside and he was fairly certain his father was there discussing the sale of the property with Mr. Tidwell at this very moment. "No. I will tell him." As the executive director, he would have to start asserting his authority—and his father seemed like the best place to start.

"Fine." She let out a contented sigh. "I will sleep well tonight, my dear, knowing Bee Tree Hill is once again in the hands of someone who will love it and use it for the purpose it was created—a home. I hope your Miss Gordon will be pleased."

"She will be more than pleased." Chase couldn't wait to tell Joy the good news. He couldn't think of a more perfect gift to offer her when he told her he loved her and asked her to marry him—something he should have followed through with four years ago. "I will talk to you soon about the reunion."

"I look forward to it, Chase. Good night."

"Good night." He tapped the red icon and slipped his phone back in his pocket. He wanted to run to Joy and the children, pull them all into his arms and tell them they never had to fear leaving Bee Tree Hill again—but first, he would have to talk to his father.

His good mood slipped and he had to square his shoulders. It would not be a pleasant conversation, and his father might never speak to him again, but Chase was willing to do whatever was necessary for his family.

He walked over the uneven lawn and down the hill toward the carriage house. The fireflies continued to dance and the sound of the band drifted on the breeze to Chase's ears. He took the stairs up to the apartment above the garage two at a time and opened the door into the kitchen.

His father sat at the table with Mr. Tidwell, several pieces of paper before them.

"Chase." His father looked up, a scowl on his face. "What time is the band done playing?"

"Ten o'clock."

"Make it nine. Mr. Tidwell and I have an early plane to catch in the morning."

Chase closed the door behind him and walked toward the table. All his life, his father had dictated his moves—but not anymore. "The city allows music to be played until ten o'clock."

"I own this property."

Sighing, Chase put his hands on the back of the chair. "Actually, the family owns this property."

"What?"

"Mr. Tidwell, will you please excuse us once again? I need to speak to my father privately."

"Of course." Mr. Tidwell rose and gathered up a few pieces of paper.

Malcolm also rose and sent a scathing look in Chase's direction before he turned a charming smile to Tidwell. "I will have all the contracts drawn up tonight and we'll sign them tomorrow before we leave for the airport."

"That's fine. Good night." Tidwell left the kitchen.

"What now?" Malcolm asked Chase, crossing his arms. "Have you come to your senses?"

Chase straightened his back and faced his father. "I just spoke to Aunt Constance."

Malcolm rolled his eyes. "I'm sure she has an opinion

about what will happen with the family antiques here at Bee Tree Hill."

It didn't pay to make this last longer than necessary. Chase wanted to tell Joy the good news as soon as possible.

"Aunt Constance has spoken to all the Asher family members," Chase said, "and they have come to a decision about Bee Tree Hill."

Malcolm narrowed his eyes, but didn't say anything.

"They have each pledged a substantial amount of money to start a trust fund for the property and they want to keep it in the family. They plan to start a nonprofit organization to minister to the widows and orphans in Timber Falls, and they have asked me to be the executive director of the estate and the organization."

"What?"

"Aunt Constance called the board of directors at the Asher Corporation to tell them her plans for the estate— you will not be authorized to sell the property without their consent."

Malcolm worked his jaw back and forth as he watched Chase. For the first time in Chase's life, his father could not control the outcome of a situation. It must be infuriating for him.

Chase took a step toward his father, hoping to salvage some kind of relationship. "I still hope we can continue—"

"Stop." Malcolm put up his hand. "It looks like you've won. I will accept their decision and leave immediately."

"You don't have to leave." Chase shook his head. "I want you to stay and get to know Joy and the kids bet—"

"No. I will tell Mr. Tidwell that the plans have changed. We will return to Minneapolis tonight and stay at a hotel."

"That's not necessary, Dad. You're always welcome at Bee Tree Hill. It's just as much your home as it is mine."

"I want nothing to do with this place a moment longer." He started to move past Chase, so Chase stepped aside.

"I hope you change your mind."

"I won't." He stopped close to Chase. "Tidwell and I will be gone in the next twenty minutes and you will not see me at Bee Tree Hill ever again."

It felt like his father's last ultimatum.

"I love you, Dad," Chase said slowly. "But I am a grown man and I need to make the best decisions I can for my own children. I'm staying in Timber Falls. I just hope you can come to terms with that choice."

His father stared at him for a moment, and then said, "We'll see." With that, he turned and left the kitchen.

It wasn't what Chase had hoped for, but at least it was a start.

Now he had a much more enjoyable conversation ahead of him, and he chose to think about that, instead.

Chapter Seventeen

The festival was coming to an end, and with it, the last evening she might have at Bee Tree Hill. A cool breeze blew across Joy's face as she walked through the upper lawn of the estate. Soft music encircled the remaining group of friends, neighbors and strangers who had stayed for the dance. She smiled at them as she passed, thankful for their love and contribution to her dream.

Mrs. Anderson still sat under the tent near the entrance to the property, a lantern offering her light. Her husband stood nearby, tapping his toe to the music as Mrs. Anderson wrote on a piece of paper.

"Joy," Mr. Anderson said when she was close. "This has been one of the nicest days I can remember. Thank you for opening your home to all of us. It's the first time I've felt a real connection with Timber Falls' history."

It probably wouldn't be her home for much longer, but she understood his sentiment. "I'm glad," she said instead. "I hope everyone remembers how important the Asher family has been to Timber Falls."

"I'm just about finished tallying these numbers," Mrs. Anderson said from her spot at the table. She scratched a few more numbers on the sheet of paper and then folded it in half. She stood and stretched, and then took a bank envelope off the table and handed it to Joy with the sheet of paper.

"Thank you for all your help today," Joy said with deep appreciation. "I don't know what I would have done without you and everyone else who helped."

"Oh, I'm happy to do it, dear." She patted Joy's cheek.

"If you're all done with her," Mr. Anderson said, extending his hand toward his wife, "I think I'll take my bride to the dance floor."

"Please," Joy said, "enjoy yourself."

Mrs. Anderson smiled and slipped her hand into her husband's as they walked off to enjoy the remaining festivities.

The piece of paper in Joy's hand held the final count the festival had earned. Joy knew down to the last penny how much she still needed to match the amount the assessor had valued the property at—and she knew it would be practically impossible that the festival had earned that much money. But the seed of hope still flourished in her heart and she took a deep breath before she opened the paper.

Headlights flashed in her eyes and she had to turn her head away from the bright light.

Mr. Asher's silver BMW crested the top of the hill and moved slowly around the circular drive. Several people had to step aside to let the vehicle pass, and everyone on the dance floor stopped dancing.

Frowning, Joy watched as the car came around the circle and passed by her.

Malcolm Asher glared at her from inside his car, but he did not slow down or stop.

Joy's heart pounded at the sight of his car leaving the property. It was too dark to see who sat beside him—but the memory of the last time he left Bee Tree Hill flooded her with the guilt and shame he had inflicted upon her. He'd accused her of horrible things both times she'd faced him—but this time, she was prepared for the hurt he caused—almost expected it. If Chase was in that car with him, or if he wasn't too far behind in his rented Jeep, Joy wouldn't allow his betrayal to cut her so deeply this time. She would be a pillar of strength for her children.

But even as she told herself those things, she didn't believe them. Pain sliced through her like it had last time, causing her legs to grow weak.

What if Chase left again? What would she tell her daughters? They knew he was their daddy—she could never change that. Had she been foolish to tell them the truth?

The car turned out of the property, and the dancing resumed, but Joy was still shook up. She couldn't think about Malcolm Asher or what had happened in the past. She had to think about her current problem—and that was housing.

Shifting aside all the pain and confusion, she took the seat Mrs. Anderson had just occupied and finally opened the sheet of paper to look at the total amount.

A staggering number was written on the paper. In all her wildest dreams, she couldn't imagine the festival raising such a sum of money, and she had each and every person there to thank.

Yet it wasn't nearly enough, just as she'd expected.

Despite her best efforts, and all the work she and Chase had done to save Bee Tree Hill, she had run out of time and didn't have enough money to buy the property.

She had tried to prepare herself for this moment—tried to keep her chin up and her hope alive—but the feeling of defeat and disappointment was strong and swift. She had let down the children, and would now have to move them to a different home, even though she had promised herself that she wouldn't raise them the way she had been raised, going from home to home.

At least she had the farmhouse to think about.

Her phone dinged and she pulled it from her pocket. A text from Tom stared back at her with more bad news. Her offer had not been accepted.

Tears burned in her eyes and she forced herself to take a deep breath. God wouldn't abandon her and the children now. If He didn't want her to have the farmhouse, then He must have a better plan.

A neighbor waved at Joy from the dance floor, laughing and smiling. Other people on the edge of the floor swayed to the music. Ryan, Jordan and Kodi played tag in the shadows of the lawn, and the light in the girls' bedroom was burning bright where their babysitters had taken them to get ready for bed.

But it was Chase, walking across the lawn, who caught and held her attention. He was so confident and comfortable here at Bee Tree Hill. He greeted those he passed with a nod or a quick hello—but he didn't stop to talk to anyone.

Instead, he walked with purpose toward Joy. He wore a pair of khaki pants and a loose button-down shirt, rolled at the sleeves.

He was still on the estate—he hadn't left with his father—and by the purpose and determination in his walk, it didn't look like he was leaving anytime soon.

There wasn't a man in Timber Falls who was as handsome as Chase, and she wished, with all her heart, that she didn't love him like she did. It was too hard to guard her heart from him. He had won it, just like before, and she had no one to blame but herself.

Joy stood when he drew near. They were removed from the dance floor, under the shadows of the tent, with only a soft lantern for light, but the sound of the music still swirled around her.

"I've been looking all over for you," Chase said tenderly, his blue eyes full of immeasurable joy. There was a glow about him that she didn't understand.

"Mrs. Anderson tallied up the final amount." Joy swallowed the truth that tried to choke her. "We failed. There isn't enough money here to save Bee Tree Hill."

"We didn't fail, Joy."

She frowned. "What do you mean? We can't possibly buy this place."

He took a step closer to her, a gentle smile tugging up his lips. "Even if we wanted to, it's no longer for sale."

Joy couldn't meet his gaze as disappointment surged through her. His father must have completed the sale with the investor and that's why they left. But why was Chase so happy? Wasn't he as disappointed as her? Or had his help these past few weeks been a ploy to manipulate her?

"I suppose you'll be going back to Seattle then," she said coolly. Was that why he was so pleased?

"I can't go back to Seattle. I made a promise to you and the kids." He gently lifted her face until she looked him in the eyes. "I plan to stay in Timber Falls permanently, just like I said."

"What about your father? Didn't he make you choose?"

"I told him I choose you and the girls—and the boys, if they want me."

Joy could hardly believe what he was saying. "Y-you choose us?"

He nodded. "Every day for the rest of my life."

The love she felt for him expanded until it overwhelmed her and she had to bite her bottom lip to keep it from trembling.

"I love you, Joy," he said, taking another step closer to her. "I never stopped loving you." He ran his thumb over her cheek and wiped away a tear she hadn't noticed. "I'm sorry about the past. If I could go back and change what happened, I would. But all I can change now is the future." He put his other hand on her other cheek and looked deep into her eyes. "Will you marry me and let me love you for the rest of my life?"

In the past, Joy would have doubted his words—doubted his intentions and promise—but now, knowing he had chosen her and the children over his father and his life in Seattle, she allowed her heart to open to him like never before.

With more tears, Joy nodded. "Yes," she whispered. "I will."

His smile was wide and glorious. He lowered his lips and kissed her like he used to. His lips were sweet, yet firm and he wrapped her in his arms as he caressed her mouth with his own. It felt like no time had passed since he'd last kissed her.

It didn't bother her if anyone watched. She loved Chase Asher and she didn't care if everyone in Timber Falls knew the truth.

Pulling away, she smiled up at him and spoke the words she'd longed to say for years. "I love you, Chase."

"I love you, too, Joy."

Suddenly, nothing else mattered. Even though they hadn't saved Bee Tree Hill, they had saved their relationship and their little family.

"You've given me the greatest gift of my life," Chase said, nodding toward the boys and then looking up at the girls' room. "The children." He held her close, the awe in his eyes endearing him to her even more. "So now I want to give you a gift—though it pales in comparison."

Curious, she waited quietly for him to continue.

"Several of my family members have pooled together their resources to save Bee Tree Hill," he said. "They are creating a trust fund to pay for the maintenance and upkeep of the property, and they are also starting a non-profit organization to help widows and orphans in Timber Falls."

Joy stared at him, trying to process what he had said.

"And they've asked me to stay here and be the executive director of the estate and organization."

"You get to stay at Bee Tree Hill?" She could hardly believe what he was saying.

"*We* get to stay," he corrected, bending down to rest his forehead against hers. "For as long as we like. This property belongs to the Asher family and that's exactly who we are."

A feeling started to grow within Joy that she had never felt before. A sense of belonging budded and then quickly bloomed. She would be a part of the most respected and well-established family in Timber Falls. No longer would she be known as the abandoned, unwanted child of her past—from now on, she would be an Asher because Chase loved her and she loved him.

The remnants of a sermon by Pastor Jacob filled her mind, and she realized that taking on the Asher name, and being welcomed into a family—not by birth, but by choice—was like being welcomed into the family of God. All the old passed away and the new was upon her.

But, more importantly, she and Chase would honor God with their marriage and their dedication to their children and to each other. Together, with the help of his family, they would minister to the needs of children in

Timber Falls—children like Ryan, Jordan and Kodi—children like Joy had once been.

"Will you allow me to adopt the boys with you when the time comes?" he asked. "I want to be their forever dad, too."

She didn't think she could love Chase any more than she already did, but his question made her melt into his arms. "Yes," she said. "I would love that and they would, too."

"Let's go tell them now," Chase said.

"Must we go right now?" Joy asked with a smile. "Can I have you to myself for a few more minutes?"

Chase grinned and then kissed her again.

This time, she didn't pull away.

Dappled sunshine paved the grass as Chase left the carriage house for the last time as a single man and walked to the base of Bee Tree Hill. There, on the lower lawn, his friends and family had gathered to witness the wedding vows he and Joy would exchange.

They couldn't have ordered a more perfect day. Just beyond the white chairs and the vine-covered trellis, the Mississippi River flowed at a lazy pace. August had arrived in Minnesota, and with it, long, sunny days and cool, starry nights.

Chase joined Pastor Jacob, who waited under the trellis.

"Are you ready?" Jacob asked Chase with a confident smile.

Nodding, Chase shook the pastor's hand. "More than ready."

In the few short months Chase had been in Timber Falls, he and the pastor had become good friends, and

Chase looked forward to strengthening that friendship as the years passed.

Chase turned to face the guests who had gathered, and he had to take a deep breath to quell the emotions that arose in his chest. There, in the front row, his mother sat next to his aunt Constance and several other family members who had come to Bee Tree Hill to set up the organization that Chase would soon manage. It seemed like a perfect time to have a family wedding, as well.

Malcolm Asher has chosen not to attend, though he had been asked. Chase could only pray that their relationship would be mended over time. He and Joy had committed to praying for him and did it often.

But today wasn't a day to look back at past regrets. Instead, Chase looked forward with every shred of hope and love he possessed. Almost everyone from their church had come out to support the couple. Chase smiled at several familiar faces, marveling that he had been welcomed into the community and church so quickly.

How was it possible to feel like he had lived here all his life?

Part of it was his connection to his family—but the biggest part was the community's respect and admiration for Joy.

Mrs. Thompson wiped tears off her cheeks as she grinned at Chase. She wore a pretty pink dress and was seated in the front row, opposite from Chase's mother. For all intents and purposes, she was Joy's mother today.

As a gentle breeze ruffled the leaves overhead, a harpist and a violinist started to play "Canon in D," and the guests rose from their chairs to turn and look up the hill.

Kinsley and Harper appeared first, wearing matching white dresses, one with a pink sash and one with a purple. Their hair had been curled and they wore shiny new shoes. The girls smiled shyly at the group as they dropped rose petals while descending the stairs. Almost at the same moment, they noticed Chase and their big brown eyes shone bright. Kinsley took Harper's hand and pulled her sister down the steps at a fast clip. They reached the lawn and Kinsley started to run down the aisle—but Harper pulled her to a stop and said very loudly, "No, Kinney, we drop the flowers first."

Harper did her job—but Kinsley couldn't wait. She raced up the aisle toward Chase and wrapped her arms around his legs. When she looked up at him, she said, "We get married today, Daddy?"

"Yes, Kinney," Chase said, resting his hand on her brown curls, "we're all getting married today."

A hush fell over the group as Joy appeared with Ryan, Jordan and Kodi on either side of her. When the boys had heard them talking about who would give away the bride, they had eagerly volunteered, and Joy had accepted with tears of happiness.

Chase could not take his eyes off his bride. She looked stunning in a white gown and veil. It was simple and elegant, just like her. She met Chase's gaze and her cheeks filled with color—but it was the love in her eyes that made his emotions finally spill over.

He couldn't believe how God had orchestrated their love story, but thinking back, he couldn't imagine it any other way. He and Joy were meant to be, and despite all the pain and heartache, their love was stronger and more powerful than ever before.

Joy walked slowly down the steps, and then down the aisle where Harper's petals were waiting for her. Kinsley jumped up and down when she saw her mama, and Chase's chest filled with the most indescribable love he had ever felt.

Finally, Joy reached his side with a smile reserved only for him.

"Who gives this bride away?" Pastor Jacob asked.

"We do!" all five children said enthusiastically.

The guests chuckled and Joy blushed. Chase stored it all away in his heart, knowing he would recall this as the best day of his life.

With the children standing around them, Chase took Joy's hand in his and pledged his life to hers. He didn't think he'd remember the words they spoke, or the sermon Jacob delivered, but he would never forget the day he, Joy and the children became a forever family, for better, for worse, for richer, for poorer, in sickness and in health, until the end of their days.

"I now pronounce you husband and wife," Pastor Jacob said at the end of the ceremony. "You may kiss your bride."

Chase took Joy into his arms and sealed the covenant with a kiss that left the children cheering, the guests applauding and Joy blushing.

"Welcome to the family, Joy Asher," he whispered to her.

The smile she offered was unlike anything he'd ever seen.

"Welcome home, Chase." Joy laced her fingers through his. "I'm so happy you came back."

Chase held his wife close as their children wrapped their arms around them in a group hug. "So am I."

He and Joy laughed and picked up the girls, and drew the boys close.

They would take pictures, eat a delicious meal and dance to the sound of a stringed orchestra under the beautiful white lights hanging in the trees. And when everyone finally left, they would tuck their children into bed and begin to live as husband and wife. It was the most marvelous way he could think of spending the rest of his life.

Just thinking about the day he had arrived at Bee Tree Hill, with plans to say goodbye to a chapter in his family's history and a piece of his past, made him cringe. Thankfully, God had a different plan. Instead of saying goodbye, he had found a new purpose for his life and for the estate. He had discovered a bright future with Joy at Bee Tree Hill and said hello to a life full of hope and meaning. He looked forward to serving the community that had given so much to the Asher family.

With Joy and the children by his side, he couldn't wait to begin.

* * * * *

Dear Reader,

It has been a joy to set *A Mother's Secret* in the fictional town of Timber Falls, inspired by my hometown on the banks of the Mississippi River. In real life, Bee Tree Hill is better known to us locals as Linden Hill, and instead of one mansion, there are actually two mansions on the nine-acre property built by lumber barons in the 1890s. Today, the estate is operated as a conference and retreat center and offers tours throughout the year. Linden Hill is especially dear to me because my dad was the caretaker for the property before the last family member passed away, and we lived in the carriage house. It was a beautiful place to grow up, and every bit of Bee Tree Hill is exactly as you'd find Linden Hill today. I hope you enjoyed spending time with me in Timber Falls.

Gabrielle Meyer

**WE HOPE YOU ENJOYED
THIS BOOK FROM**

LOVE INSPIRED
INSPIRATIONAL ROMANCE

Uplifting stories of faith, forgiveness and hope.

Fall in love with stories where faith helps
guide you through life's challenges, and discover
the promise of a new beginning.

6 NEW BOOKS AVAILABLE EVERY MONTH!

LIHALO2020

COMING NEXT MONTH FROM
Love Inspired

Available February 18, 2020

THE AMISH TEACHER'S DILEMMA
North Country Amish • by Patricia Davids

Taking a schoolteacher position in another district was just the change Amish spinster Eva Coblentz needed. But with her family insisting she come home just as she falls for three troubled orphans and their guardian uncle, Willis Gingrich, will she return to her old life...or risk everything to build a new one?

HEALING THEIR AMISH HEARTS
Colorado Amish Courtships • by Leigh Bale

Becca Graber has made it her mission to get the silent boy in her new classroom to speak again. But she's not quite sure *why* he doesn't talk. Working with the child's father, widower Jesse King, can she break through to little Sam...and begin to repair all their broken hearts?

FINDING THE ROAD HOME
Hearts of Oklahoma • by Tina Radcliffe

With potential budget cuts looming, police chief Mitch Rainbolt may have to let his latest hire go—unless he and officer Daisy Anderson can prove that their department deserves the money. Can they save her job...and ensure Daisy and her orphaned nieces and nephews stay in town for good?

THE TEXAN'S PROMISE
Cowboys of Diamondback Ranch • by Jolene Navarro

To save her ranch, Belle De La Rosa must sell part of it to developers—and only conservationist Quinn Sinclair stands in her way. Belle can't help but feel drawn to the widower and his children, but will she take a chance on love even when she finds out his true reason for being in town?

THE COWBOY'S UNEXPECTED BABY
Triple Creek Cowboys • by Stephanie Dees

When rancher and attorney Garrett Cole finds a newborn baby on his doorstep, he has no idea how to even change a diaper. Help comes in the form of Abby Scott, his new temporary coworker. But can Garrett convince Abby she'd be the perfect permanent addition to his makeshift family?

HER SECRET TWINS
by Janette Foreman

Kallie Shore's late father knew she couldn't raise her girls *and* work the family farm alone. But the plan he specified in his will isn't the one she'd have chosen: Kallie inherits half the farm, but the other half goes to Grant Young, her ex-fiancé...and the secret father of her twins.

LOOK FOR THESE AND OTHER LOVE INSPIRED BOOKS WHEREVER BOOKS ARE SOLD, INCLUDING MOST BOOKSTORES, SUPERMARKETS, DISCOUNT STORES AND DRUGSTORES.

LICNM0220

SPECIAL EXCERPT FROM

🌿

LOVE INSPIRED
INSPIRATIONAL ROMANCE

*Can the new teacher in this Amish community help the
family next door without losing her heart?*

Read on for a sneak preview of
The Amish Teacher's Dilemma *by Patricia Davids,
available in March 2020 from Love Inspired.*

Clang, clang, clang.

The hammering outside her new schoolhouse grew
louder. Eva Coblentz moved to the window to locate
the source of the clatter. Across the road she saw a man
pounding on an ancient-looking piece of machinery with
steel wheels and a scoop-like nose on the front end.

When he had the sheet of metal shaped to fit the front
of the machine, he stood back to assess his work. He
knelt and hammered on the shovel-like nose three more
times. Satisfied, he gathered up his tools and started in
her direction.

She stepped back from the window. Was he coming to
the school? Why? Had he noticed her gawking? Perhaps
he only wanted to welcome the new teacher, although his
lack of a beard said he wasn't married.

She glanced around the room. Should she meet him
by the door? That seemed too eager. Her eyes settled on
the large desk at the front of the classroom. She should
look as if she was ready for the school year to start. A
professional attitude would put off any suggestion that
she was interested in meeting single men.

Eva hurried to the desk, pulled out the chair and sat down as the outside door opened. The chair tipped over backward, sending her flailing. Her head hit the wall with a painful thud as she slid to the floor. Stunned, she slowly opened her eyes to see the man leaning over the desk.

He had the most beautiful gray eyes she'd ever beheld. They were rimmed with thick, dark lashes in stark contrast to the mop of curly, dark red hair springing out from beneath his straw hat. Tiny sparks of light whirled around him.

"I'm Willis Gingrich. Local blacksmith." He squatted beside her. "Can you tell me your name?"

The warmth and strength of his hand on her skin sent a sizzle of awareness along her nerve endings. "I'm Eva Coblentz. I am the new teacher and I'm fine now."

Don't miss
The Amish Teacher's Dilemma
by USA TODAY *bestselling author Patricia Davids,*
available March 2020 wherever
Love Inspired books and ebooks are sold.

LoveInspired.com

Copyright © 2020 by Patricia MacDonald

LIEXP0220

Get 4 FREE REWARDS!

We'll send you 2 FREE Books plus 2 FREE Mystery Gifts.

Love Inspired books feature uplifting stories where faith helps guide you through life's challenges and discover the promise of a new beginning.

The Wrangler's Last Chance
JESSICA KELLER

Their Wander Canyon Wish
ALLIE PLEITER

FREE
Value Over
$20

YES! Please send me 2 FREE Love Inspired Romance novels and my 2 FREE mystery gifts (gifts are worth about $10 retail). After receiving them, if I don't wish to receive any more books, I can return the shipping statement marked "cancel." If I don't cancel, I will receive 6 brand-new novels every month and be billed just $5.24 each for the regular-print edition or $5.99 each for the larger-print edition in the U.S., or $5.74 each for the regular-print edition or $6.24 each for the larger-print edition in Canada. That's a savings of at least 13% off the cover price. It's quite a bargain! Shipping and handling is just 50¢ per book in the U.S. and $1.25 per book in Canada.* I understand that accepting the 2 free books and gifts places me under no obligation to buy anything. I can always return a shipment and cancel at any time. The free books and gifts are mine to keep no matter what I decide.

Choose one: ☐ **Love Inspired Romance Regular-Print** (105/305 IDN GNWC) ☐ **Love Inspired Romance Larger-Print** (122/322 IDN GNWC)

Name (please print)

Address   Apt. #

City   State/Province   Zip/Postal Code

Mail to the **Reader Service:**
IN U.S.A.: P.O. Box 1341, Buffalo, NY 14240-8531
IN CANADA: P.O. Box 603, Fort Erie, Ontario L2A 5X3

Want to try 2 free books from another series! Call 1-800-873-8635 or visit www.ReaderService.com.

*Terms and prices subject to change without notice. Prices do not include sales taxes, which will be charged (if applicable) based on your state or country of residence. Canadian residents will be charged applicable taxes. Offer not valid in Quebec. This offer is limited to one order per household. Books received may not be as shown. Not valid for current subscribers to Love Inspired Romance books. All orders subject to approval. Credit or debit balances in a customer's account(s) may be offset by any other outstanding balance owed by or to the customer. Please allow 4 to 6 weeks for delivery. Offer available while quantities last.

Your Privacy—The Reader Service is committed to protecting your privacy. Our Privacy Policy is available online at www.ReaderService.com or upon request from the Reader Service. We make a portion of our mailing list available to reputable third parties that offer products we believe may interest you. If you prefer that we not exchange your name with third parties, or if you wish to clarify or modify your communication preferences, please visit us at www.ReaderService.com/consumerchoice or write to us at Reader Service Preference Service, P.O. Box 9062, Buffalo, NY 14240-9062. Include your complete name and address.

LI20R